THE RELUCTANT BRIDE

Natalie Kleinman

SAPERE
BOOKS

THE RELUCTANT BRIDE

Published by Sapere Books.

20 Windermere Drive, Leeds, England, LS17 7UZ,
United Kingdom

saperebooks.com

ISBN: 978-1-80055-119-0

ACKNOWLEDGEMENTS

So many people have helped me on this journey that it's hard to know who to thank first, and there is always the risk of leaving someone out. I apologise in advance if that's the case. So, in no particular order, to Amy Durant and all the team at Sapere Books who have gone above and beyond the call to get me to this point. They have supported me in ways that I would never have expected from a publisher. The weekly Zoom meetings with the Sapere 'stable' of authors where I have made friends and learned so much. And speaking of much learning, Elaine Everest, friend, owner and tutor at The Write Place creative writing school, to whom I owe more than I can say. Jean Gilardi, Moya Goatley and Bren Eastwood whose daily exchange of emails over many years have been an invaluable support. My sister, Rhona Cohen, who is always ready to bounce ideas around with me and who keeps me daily supplied with crossword puzzles. My children, Carole Whyley and Tracy Harris, who are proud of me as only children can be. My husband, Louis, who is always ready to read my work and is wonderful at discovering typos. I couldn't ask for more support than he willingly gives me. Well, he seems to give it willingly. I come at last to my inspiration, Georgette Heyer, without whom this book would never have been written. I hope it honours her.

PROLOGUE

"But Papa, he's almost forty years old," Charlotte protested when her father told her she was to marry Ernest, Earl of Cranleigh.

Sir Archibald Willoughby shifted uncomfortably but stuck to his guns. "Hardly a stripling, I know, but an older man will be good for you. He will perhaps curb your tendency towards levity." The accusation was unjust, for even though Charlotte possessed a lively sense of humour she understood her responsibilities. But this was one obligation that struck fear into her heart. "A girl your age can't afford to set people's backs up, you know."

"But I hardly know him. I've only met him twice."

"You must nevertheless be aware of his interest in you. Once he learned of your shared passion for horses, Lord Cranleigh came to Stapleton with the sole desire of being presented to you. There's no understanding it to be sure, though we must be grateful it is the case, but it seems for him to be sufficient reason to consider an alliance. The Earl desires an heir. You should be honoured that he considers you suitable to fulfil that role."

"Papa, I couldn't!" Charlotte pleaded, horrified by the thought. "My affections are not engaged!"

"What do affections matter where duty is involved?" Sir Archibald said tersely, before softening his voice. "Come now, Charlotte, you of all people know how things stand with us. The Earl will be kind to you, I am sure. And just think, you will be the Countess of Cranleigh with all the advantages that title carries. Consider your own position. You are not exactly in your first bloom. It is time almost to turn your sister Harriet off."

"Then let *her* marry Cranleigh!" Charlotte retorted, displaying a spirit that her father, a weak man, habitually found difficult to cope with.

Sir Archibald resorted to bluster. "You are being foolish beyond permission. Naturally you must marry first."

Charlotte begged and beseeched but, as the elder daughter of an impoverished father, she knew it fell to her to rescue the family from the penury that threatened. Ernest had pledged to settle Sir Archibald's debts and to make good the estate which had suffered from the ravages of time and neglect. Naturally, her parent did not discuss the finer details of any settlements with her, but the Earl would make generous provision for his bride. And for her father.

"Above all," Sir Archibald said, pressing home his point, "Cranleigh will save the good name of our family. I will brook no disobedience. You *will* marry the Earl. And I will not discuss this matter any further."

Within a month, Charlotte was married. After the initial shock of the ceremony, Charlotte was able to relax into her new life. The house in St James's Square was everything she could have wished. It warmed her to see so lovely a home having the care lavished upon it that once, long ago, had been evident at Stapleton. She was given her own apartments and the freedom to do with them as she wished.

Ernest was so considerate and easy to like that Charlotte found it no hardship spending time in his company. A growing respect for her husband helped Charlotte adjust to her new situation. Unable to buck fate that had dictated she marry without love, she was determined to make her new life as comfortable as she could.

But then her world was turned upside down once more. In an attempt to impress his peers, Ernest had over-faced his horse. Four hooves dug in and the horse ground to a halt. Not so Ernest, who cleared the fence with feet to spare but met his demise on landing when his head struck a large boulder.

Six weeks after her marriage, the Countess of Cranleigh was a widow.

CHAPTER ONE

"Oh, do come for a walk, Charlotte. No-one would condemn you for taking the air on such a day. Surely your widow's weeds are token enough of your mourning. There can be no impropriety."

Charlotte looked up at her younger sister. It was now eleven months since Ernest's accident, and Charlotte's formal period of mourning had seemed endless. After much resistance from Sir Archibald, Harriet and their cousin Esther had been allowed to join Charlotte as companions. "My widow's weeds lie, Harriet," Charlotte remarked ruefully. "I am sad, of course, for Ernest was a nice man, but I do not mourn in the usual way, nor could you expect me to."

"Indeed not, but it is what the world believes."

"Yes, much of it, at any rate, and I must maintain the deception."

"But you do not have to maintain it by sitting all day at your needlework."

Appreciating the logic of Harriet's remark, Charlotte laid aside the offending stitchery and rose to her feet, her natural enthusiasm once more to the fore. "You're right, Harriet," she said, her voice already lighter at the anticipated treat. "I shall fetch my bonnet and we will stroll around the square."

Pausing only to tell Esther of their plans, the two young women prepared to leave the house.

"Don't you go catching a chill now," scolded Esther. "Spring is barely upon us and I don't trust that wind."

Charlotte laughed at her. "No-one would ever take you for a country-woman, Esther. Why, when we were children you were the first person to send us out into the fresh air because it was good for us."

"That's all you know. It was to get you out from under my feet. Go on, then. Off with you. Take a shawl, though, if only to satisfy a fussy old woman."

Esther, approaching forty, was neither old nor fussy, but had stood as mother to them since their own had died when they were still very small. Younger than Emily Willoughby by only a few years, Esther had stepped in to care for her cousins, having no closer family of her own to consider. Harriet barely remembered her parent, but Charlotte could still picture the beautiful woman seated at her dressing-table, putting the finishing touches to her *toilette* but ready to crush her fine silks to embrace her children.

When Lady Willoughby had been carried off by an infection, Sir Archibald had indulged in every sort of extravagance and exploit in an attempt to soften his grief. Sadly, his loss hadn't encouraged him to spend time with two small girls. Moreover, having always been a distant father, he withdrew from them almost entirely, leaving them to the care of his household.

Esther had provided the love their father had not. If she was slightly outspoken in company, this certainly didn't bother her charges and they would have dismissed any criticism of her as unacceptable. She might spoil and scold in equal measure in the privacy of their home, but in public she would take care that no unwelcome attention would disturb Lady Cranleigh or Miss Willoughby.

"It seems Esther was right about the shawl," Charlotte remarked, stepping out from the house and hugging her own around her slight frame.

"It's so good to be outdoors. I never thought I'd say it, Charlotte, but I'd love to be back home, striding across the fields with the wind in my hair and none to reprimand me for a tomboy. Yet remember how I used to yearn to visit London?"

"And if you were even now at Stapleton, no doubt you would yearn again. I know what you mean, though. London ladies seem not to appreciate the pleasure of a good brisk walk."

Turning to their left at the bottom of the steps, the sisters increased their pace as they entered St James's Square, completely unconscious of the charming picture they presented, the one with hair the colour of the gleaming nut for which it was named, the other of sun-kissed straw.

Two turns around the square and the fidgets which had so irked Harriet, and Charlotte too would she but own it, had flown away on the breeze. With roses in their cheeks, the young ladies climbed the few steps to their house to be greeted by a footman.

"The Duke of Gresham has called to see you, my Lady," he told Charlotte. "I showed him to the morning room."

"Thank you, Barnes," Charlotte replied, stiffening at the news. She removed her bonnet as she spoke and handed it to him. "Come, Harriet, we mustn't keep His Grace waiting any longer," she said with a slight edge to her voice.

There had only been two dutiful visits from Gresham since the death of her husband. Ernest had left Charlotte well-provided-for, but his title and estates went to Gresham, though what use another and lesser title could be to him, Charlotte had no idea. Nor did she care. What annoyed her was the timing of this visit. A certain etiquette was lacking. After an initial morning call shortly after her husband's death, and the one that had succeeded it sometime later, convention dictated that he ought to have called again at least once in the ensuing months. He hadn't done so.

With her sister behind her, Charlotte climbed the imposing oak staircase to the first floor, glancing as she did so at a portrait of her husband. It displayed an aristocratic but kindly face and gave her pause for a moment, causing her to smile as she remembered his understanding and forbearance. Her own likeness had been commissioned before his death, but this had been abandoned as she couldn't feel it appropriate for her to sit at this time. Charlotte stood outside the door, preparing herself to meet a very different man from Ernest and, taking a deep breath, she grasped the handle firmly and entered the room with Harriet in her wake. A vision of perfect manhood turned from where he stood, his hand resting on the mantelshelf, his foot on the hearth. Not a crease could she see in his fine clothes. She felt sure, had she been close enough, that she would have been able to see her reflection in the polish of his boots.

"Good morning, Your Grace," she said, moving towards him and extending her hand in greeting. "It is very kind of you to call. Please allow me to introduce my sister, Miss Willoughby. I believe she was not at home when last you came."

The words were all they should have been, but Gresham would have to have been a fool not to detect the undertone that accompanied them, and Charlotte was quite sure he was not a fool. There was a certain acuity, something in his expression that told her he was aware of her disapproval and, annoyingly, that he was amused by it. He took the proffered hand, holding it for just the correct amount of time, and bowed before turning from her to Harriet, repeating the gesture.

"You must forgive me, ladies. I have been out of town for some months now, returning but briefly from time to time. Consequently, I am only now able to pay this long overdue visit. Allow me once again to offer you my sincere condolences. Ernest was a good man."

Charlotte was mortified. Indignation had been building up inside her for so long that she had annoyingly allowed it to show. Not only that, but Gresham glanced at her uncovered hair and, though he looked away again quickly, she had seen the raised eyebrow. In her haste to greet her visitor, Charlotte had forgotten when she removed her bonnet that she was not wearing her widow's cap. About to explain, she bit back the words. She was dashed if she would apologise to this man whose aloof air spoiled an otherwise perfect image.

"Pray be seated, Your Grace. We have just this moment returned from a walk about the square. Had we been in expectation of your visit, we would naturally have remained at home."

"Naturally," he replied, a little mockingly she thought.

They exchanged pleasantries for perhaps five minutes, after which time Gresham stood up. "Pray excuse me if I cut my visit short. My man of business demands my presence. After so prolonged a spell away, there is much to catch up on."

Charlotte bit her lip. How ungentlemanly of him to press home his point so clearly. She rose also, as did Harriet.

"Then it was good of you to spare us the time. We are honoured. Thank you," said Charlotte, gazing up at him with a challenge in her face that belied the docility in her voice.

"I am always at your service, Lady Cranleigh. Please don't hesitate to let me know if at any time you require my assistance." But there was no warmth in the invitation and Charlotte was aware of Gresham's continued hostility.

"You are too kind," she replied through gritted teeth. He knew she had been wrong-footed and had enjoyed her discomfiture. And she knew that he knew.

"Insufferable!" The word burst from Charlotte as the door closed behind him.

"But handsome, Charlotte. You have to admit that."

"Yes, handsome, but nonetheless insufferable! I do not like him and he makes it very plain he does not like me!"

Unsettled by Gresham's call, Charlotte sat down to resume her needlework, but the lightness that her walk had instilled in her had dissipated with his visit. She stared out of the window with the rest of her semi-isolation seeming to stretch interminably in front of her.

Later that afternoon, with barely a stitch having been set, she looked up as her sister burst into the room.

"Lady Stanford invites us to a soirée, Charlotte. Oh do please let us go," Harriet exclaimed excitedly.

"You know I cannot attend parties for another three weeks, my darling," Charlotte replied with no little regret. "You must be patient a while longer. We both must. Or you may go with Esther if you wish." The restraint of the past several months was fast abating as she began to look forward to a freer life. The proximity of that life, though, only accentuated her restlessness.

"No, look," Harriet said, standing behind her sister, leaning over her shoulder and waving the card. "It says there will be no music or card-playing. Just a get-together for a few friends. A light supper. To ease you back into society, she says."

"Oh, how kind of Maria," Charlotte replied, her excitement all at once rising as she plucked the invitation from Harriet's fingers to see for herself. "I wonder if I ought."

"Maria Stanford would never commit a social impropriety. Of course you must go. Wait, though, I'll get Esther. You know what a stickler she is. Let's see what she has to say." Off she went to find her.

Charlotte felt something stir inside her not dissimilar to the gentle movements of a butterfly emerging from its chrysalis and spreading its wings. She had become used to her dull existence and had serious qualms (which she was of course determined to overcome) about going out into the world again. She feared she had lost the art of easy conversation. But she had her sister to think about. Along with her own confinement had come Harriet's, too kind to accept invitations that Charlotte could not.

Before her marriage, Charlotte had begun to enjoy modest social engagements in the society of those whom she had known almost from her cradle. One or two young men had shown a marked preference for her company. Charlotte felt strongly the restrictions which had removed her almost entirely from society these last few months. Having been forced into a loveless marriage, it seemed particularly cruel that she should then be forced into the appearance of a year's mourning, tacitly displaying a grief she did not feel. She had been patient, but her friend's invitation had awoken something dormant within her. Charlotte had a zest for life, and she wanted to meet it head-on. She knew what her answer was to be, even before her sister came back into the room almost dragging Esther with her.

"Tell her, Esther. Tell her it's perfectly acceptable for us to go."

"I would suggest the dove-grey silk," was their mentor's response. "It would be more than suitable for your first appearance, and just think how magnificent your hair will look against that colour," she added a little mischievously.

Charlotte responded primly, though the smile in Esther's eyes was reflected in her own. "It will be confined under a cap, as is fitting." She then spoiled the whole effect by giggling.

"Fitting indeed, when a beautiful young woman is forced to cover her crowning glory simply because it is the convention. When she should be having a good time instead of sitting demurely in a corner." Esther was indignant on her cousin's behalf, and neither of her young relatives bothered to point out that if they'd attempted to do anything outrageous she would have been the first to censure them.

"Well, I think it very thoughtful of Maria to give Charlotte this opportunity of stepping out again without having to face hundreds of people for the first time all in one go."

"Hardly hundreds, Harriet, but I agree. Maria has a kind heart and will see to it that you and Charlotte ease your way in gently."

"And you shall be there to see to it that we behave as you would expect us to."

"I? You don't need me to look after you with your hostess acting as chaperone. Indeed, your sister is of age and it is perfectly respectable for you to go under her aegis."

"Come now, Esther," Charlotte remarked. "Did you not read the invitation? There is no question but that you should accompany us. You come as our cousin, not as a chaperone. In any case, I imagine you must be feeling your constraint as keenly as we are."

There. It was out. Charlotte had admitted that she found her enforced seclusion restricting in the extreme.

"Let me see, then," Esther said, taking the card from Charlotte. "Three days! My goodness, we have much to do. Come. We will go upstairs and examine the dove-grey silk and decide what accessories you are to wear. Then Harriet, the pale yellow muslin for you, I think. It will complement your hair, and there are few girls who can wear that colour without their skin turning pasty white. You are fortunate in that you have your mother's complexion."

The three women went to Charlotte's bedchamber and spent a happy time choosing and discarding, matching and rejecting. After the long winter months, it seemed the sun was shining inside as well as out in St James's Square.

CHAPTER TWO

Charlotte sat at her dressing table, not displeased with her reflection in the glass. Her abigail had brushed and teased her hair into gleaming ringlets which no number of demure little caps could disguise. Putting her head on one side, she gasped as the very image of her mother stared back at her. But for the colour of her hair, it might have been Emily Willoughby reflected in the glass. Charlotte had always known she resembled her but had never before seen it to this degree.

Tears sprang to her eyes as she remembered the affection in which she'd been held. There had been cuddles and tickles in equal measure, Lady Willoughby's laugh like a tinkling bell. Charlotte imagined too that she could smell the familiar perfume her mother always wore.

"Oh Mama, if only you were here now to guide me. How am I to behave? Twenty-one years old and the widow of a man I did not love, though I grew to hold him in affection in our few short weeks together. Should I sit with the matrons? Am I allowed to enjoy myself? And what of Harriet, beautiful Harriet, who I am sure will take the world by storm? You'd be so proud of her. She has been a rock to me these past few months."

Mama did not reply. Charlotte would have to work it out for herself.

Harriet bounced into the room and came to an abrupt halt. "Charlotte, you look beautiful," she exclaimed. "I love what Bella has done with your hair."

Charlotte did too but couldn't help wondering if it was perhaps a bit too frivolous, and said so.

"Of course not. Stop acting like an old maid."

"The truth is, Harriet, I don't know how to act." There was an appeal in her eyes.

"Oh no! You're frightened! I didn't realise you were so nervous. Oh, my poor darling. Don't worry. We shall look after each other, and if we don't Esther definitely will."

"She'll have to," Charlotte said in an attempt to curb her uneasiness, "because she will certainly have her work cut out keeping all those beaux away from you." Her effort was rewarded as she felt her anxiety subside a little. "She was right about the yellow muslin, though. You look like a ray of sunshine."

Esther chose this moment to enter the room and exclaim, "You'll do. Yes, very nice, both of you."

"No less you, Esther. The blue muslin suits you admirably."

"Charlotte said I will be surrounded by beaux," Harriet broke in, somewhat ingenuously.

"It's a soirée, my dear. No-one will be surrounded by anyone," Esther said coolly, succeeding in pulling her young charge back down to earth a little. "Remember Maria's kind words about easing you in gently. I doubt there will be more than twenty people present in all."

The slight put-down had its effect, but nothing was really going to diminish Harriet's enthusiasm at her first proper outing in almost a year. She had appeared only a few times before her brother-in-law's accident and was then but a very green girl. During the ensuing months she had matured, and this had only succeeded in adding to her charm, for there was something appealing about her to be sure.

"Of course. I was merely funning. But I am looking forward to meeting some new people, and of course to seeing Maria again."

"Sam Coachman will be here in a few minutes. Run and fetch your pelisse, Harriet. You too, Charlotte. It wouldn't do to catch a chill on your first outing."

The three ladies, in varying states of excitement and apprehension, went out to meet the world, or a small part of it at least.

There were only some twenty persons in the room to which Charlotte, Harriet and Esther were escorted. Their hostess rose to embrace the younger ladies and to exchange greetings with their cousin.

"It's been too long, my dear. And Harriet," Lady Stanford said, turning to the younger sister, "this will be your first real season, will it not? I hope my small gathering will be a relaxing introduction for you."

Charlotte acknowledged the welcome. "We have so much appreciated your visits these past few months, Maria. You can have no idea how much light they added to our days."

"Such sad circumstances. And you so young. Well, my family and the Cranleighs have a long association and, while you may hold fond memories of your husband, it is time for you to return to the world. You are far too lovely to be hidden away. I would be derelict in my duty if I didn't do my utmost to help. Not that it is a duty," she added. "I have a great fondness for you."

Charlotte blushed, but her colour faded rapidly and she even paled slightly as she looked up to see the Duke of Gresham approaching.

"My dear Lady Cranleigh, how nice to see you again, and so soon after our last meeting. I trust I find you well."

"Indeed, sir, we are all quite well," Charlotte replied.

"Miss Willoughby, you must have long been waiting for this day," he said to Harriet. He turned to Esther. "I don't believe I've had the pleasure."

"May I make known to you Miss Meredith, Your Grace. Our cousin and dear friend." Charlotte bit her lip, cross that she had not had the opportunity of introducing Esther sooner and being made to feel again that she had been maladroit.

"Allow me to find you a seat and procure some refreshment. A glass of ratafia, or Madeira, perhaps," Gresham said, leading them to a free sofa against the far wall. His manner was almost avuncular, a side of him they had not previously been privileged to see. Charlotte caught a gleam of amusement in his eye, making her considerably more comfortable to discover that beneath his habitual air of hauteur he had a sense of humour. Could she have been wrong about him?

Charlotte watched in amusement as a tall man approached, weaving his way amongst the crowd while at the same time precariously balancing a tray in one hand.

"I begged Gresham here to allow me to help him carry the glasses, knowing how devastated he would be should he spill a drop on those fine pantaloons."

"Permit me, Peacock, to present the Countess of Cranleigh."

The man relinquished the tray into Gresham's hands and bowed to Charlotte.

"Lady Cranleigh, my dear friend, the Honourable Quentin Peacock, whose appalling lack of manners is only ameliorated by his charm. Don't listen to a word he says. The importance of my apparel fades into insignificance when set beside the desire to fulfil my quest."

"I'm delighted to meet you, Mr Peacock. How kind of you to assist the Duke in such an arduous task," Charlotte replied with a smile.

"Miss Harriet Willoughby, Lady Cranleigh's sister, and their cousin, Miss Meredith," Gresham continued, completing the formalities.

Mr Peacock pulled up a chair and lowered his large frame onto it, at the same time unconsciously brushing aside a rogue shock of fairish brown hair. "To be truthful, and though I hate to admit it, Gresham is a capable chap, perfectly able to have performed such a deed alone, but I saw you across the room and … well, I admit I hoped for an introduction."

Mr Peacock spoke to all the ladies but his eyes were for Harriet alone. She was not immune to this kind of flattery and Esther was on the alert but, though the colour in her cheeks was heightened, Harriet behaved with decorum, being neither ruffled nor school-girlish. She merely lowered her eyes demurely and accepted the compliment.

Lady Stanford had done well with her guest list, inviting an eclectic group of people, all of whom could be relied upon to put Charlotte and Harriet at their ease. Acquainted as she was with Lady Jersey, Lady Stanford had only to mention that Gresham, an old friend of her husband, would be present, to entice her to join the party. Charlotte could scarce believe at first that this ebullient lady was indeed one of the august few who held so much sway at the famous London assembly rooms. She was soon brought to change her mind, for though the countess chatted incessantly, her brilliant dark eyes were constantly on the move and it became obvious that very little escaped her.

"Your late husband and mine were friends, did you know? The Earl is a racehorse owner and I was aware of Cranleigh's passion for the sport."

"I did not know. I am aware of course of my own husband's enthusiasm, for it is the interest we shared," Charlotte replied with animation, as she always did when the talk turned to horses.

"You will be wanting vouchers for our club, you and your sister. What do you think, Gresham?" Lady Jersey asked, turning to the Duke, who had at that moment joined them. "Shall Lady Cranleigh and her sister come to Almack's? Maria," she said, hailing their hostess, "remind me to send vouchers if you will."

When Charlotte announced she was leaving, Gresham turned to her.

"Would you allow me to escort you and your sister around the square tomorrow?" he asked. "I know how much you enjoyed it the other day."

Charlotte was surprised and, to her annoyance, gratified by his suggestion, but she would not give him the satisfaction of knowing that. She raised her chin and said provocatively, "Having been away for so long, Your Grace, surely you must have a lot to do. You said as much when referring to your man of business."

"Ah, but it has been necessary for him to leave town for a few days."

"Does this not then make it even more imperative for you to apply yourself?"

"Alas, without his aid I am helpless. I beg you to rescue me from my inadequacy."

Charlotte laughed, acknowledging his wit and enjoying the banter after her months of seclusion, and appreciating this other side of a man whom she had before considered so aloof. "Well, sir, in that case we should be delighted. Perhaps your friend would like to join us."

The invitation was extended and accepted with alacrity.

CHAPTER THREE

Charlotte and Harriet stepped into St James's Square at the allotted time to find Gresham and Mr Peacock already waiting. Greetings were exchanged and Gresham invited Esther to join the party.

"Thank you, Your Grace, but there are tasks that require attending to here. Do go, all of you. It's a lovely day."

They set out after a brief discussion as to whether to turn right or left when descending the steps. Mr Peacock would have it they should go left, falling in with the main flow of pedestrians and thus avoiding the necessity of introducing his companions to any with whom they might come face to face. Charlotte suspected he was eager to keep Harriet to himself.

"It will be tedious to have to stop all the time," he said, "saying good morning to this one and how do you do to that."

But he was overruled by all three of his companions.

"I should like to meet some of your friends," Harriet said simply.

They walked two by two and Charlotte found herself quite in charity with Gresham. He was entertaining and informative in a straightforward way which she liked. When she had pointed out a beautifully matched pair of greys, saying with envy that she would wish to own such a team, it seemed they would go on very well together.

"I didn't know you were so knowledgeable about horseflesh," he remarked.

"No, how should you?" she countered, smiling up at him. "We are barely acquainted, after all."

He met her amused gaze and quickly withdrew his eyes. "You are very right. No doubt you shared your interest with Ernest."

"It was what we had most in common. I haven't ridden since I left Stapleton and I miss it sorely."

"A deprivation indeed! Do you drive as well?"

"Certainly I do, though nothing as fancy as the turnouts I am seeing today. It was necessary, before I married that is, to visit our tenants. My father was so rarely at home it fell to me to engage with them. It would never have done to go bowling around the country in a curricle or phaeton. No, a gig was what I used, when not riding, and very handy it was."

"Then perhaps you will allow me to drive you in one of my carriages from time to time. I could show you and Miss Willoughby some parts of London you have not yet had the opportunity to see."

"That is kind, Your Grace. It's something I know we would both appreciate."

Gresham began to outline various places of interest. So engrossed were they in their conversation that they almost walked into Harriet and Mr Peacock, who had stopped to exchange greetings with a pleasant-looking man.

"Ah, good morning, Fortescue. Allow me to present Miss Harriet Willoughby and the Countess of Cranleigh. And here's Gresham, their cousin."

"Yes," Gresham said, "you will remember Ernest met with an unfortunate accident, Fortescue. I have taken it upon myself as my family duty to look out for Lady Cranleigh, if she will allow me to do so."

Charlotte was startled. Duty? Was this what he was doing? She felt a momentary pang of disappointment, thinking he had liked her for herself. However, she straight away realised how helpful his patronage could be to her and to cover her let-down said, "We are naturally grateful to the Duke for his kind attention."

A few more words and the party moved on. For Charlotte, though, a little warmth had gone out of the morning. A short way along, Mr Peacock was hailed by a well-dressed man of a similar age to himself and the necessary introductions were made.

"Enchanting," said the newcomer to Charlotte, with what she considered to be inappropriate exaggeration. "It is to be hoped we will meet again soon. I shall look for you at the assemblies, if I may."

"It will be a pleasure to see you, Lord Roxburgh," Charlotte replied, not quite comfortable with the way he bent low over her hand, his lips almost touching her fingertips, but flattered nonetheless. The courtesy seemed a little old-fashioned and, in her opinion, a little forward on such short acquaintance. She thought perhaps there were some social niceties of which she was unaware and resolved to ask Esther's advice. There was, however, a certain something about the man that must always appeal to the ladies.

What surprised her was the air of disdain with which Gresham had greeted him. Almost as if he was beneath his touch. Was he so high in the instep then that this man wasn't worthy of his friendship? She was disappointed. As far as she was concerned, such blatant snobbery was another black mark against him. She concluded that her first impression about Gresham being snobbish and proud was confirmed.

So impatient was Charlotte of what she considered to be misplaced pride that she prolonged her conversation with Roxburgh beyond what she might otherwise have done. Aside from wishing to demonstrate to Gresham that good manners were a desirable trait, she was intrigued also by this newcomer who seemed more of an extrovert than those men she had previously met. It had a certain allure.

"My sister and I are hoping to re-enter society now that my period of mourning is coming to an end. No doubt our paths will cross at some function or other."

"I shall wait impatiently until then, Lady Cranleigh," Roxburgh said. "Society will be all the richer for your added presence." This, spoken as it was in an exaggerated manner, was perhaps a little more extravagant than Charlotte would have wished, especially as he allowed his lips to touch her fingers as he made his farewell.

Charlotte regretted immediately that she had encouraged him. She found him both intriguing and discomposing in equal measure.

Charlotte looked in vain for Lord Gresham during the course of the next week, for though she might deplore his arrogance she nonetheless found her exchanges with him to be stimulating.

It was Harriet, not Charlotte, who had brought up his name in conversation.

"Did the Duke not say he would drive us out in his carriage one day?"

"Yes, but no firm arrangement was made. Perhaps he hasn't had time."

"And now it will be a while, for Mr Peacock tells me he is gone out of town. A pity, as it would have been a nice outing."

Charlotte too was disappointed but wouldn't have dreamed of saying so. His assertion on the day of their walk that he was duty-bound to look after her seemed not to hold water. After their difficult start she had begun to take pleasure in his company, and though she still had reservations about him she would, she knew, miss their lively conversations.

"There will be outings enough soon, dearest. Have you seen how many invitations are assembled on the escritoire? We shall have barely a moment to ourselves if we accept even half of them."

And it was true. The number of morning callers had increased dramatically since the night of Lady Stanford's soirée. While Charlotte was still not able to attend parties or assemblies where dancing or gaming might be in progress, there could be no objection to her receiving visitors under Esther's watchful eye.

As many came to see Harriet as Charlotte, though it seemed the budding friendship between Miss Willoughby and Mr Quentin Peacock could easily turn into something stronger. At least her head would not be turned by some other totally inappropriate suitor, Esther reflected. Charlotte, however, hoped that the young couple had not privately reached an understanding. Her ambitions were all for her sister, and she felt that it would be a pity if Harriet were not to enjoy the company of several young men before settling for one, however eligible he might be.

"What do you think, Esther? Should I discourage such frequent visits?"

"By no means. I fear such action would only lower her spirits and, while Mr Peacock is particular in his attentions, he does not go beyond the bounds of what is acceptable. He has the sense, too, more often than not, to bring some friend or other with him when he calls."

"A ruse, Esther," Charlotte smiled. "He hopes I will be engaged in conversation with them and thus leave him free to dally with Harriet."

"Except he isn't dallying, is he? He seems to have quite a serious turn of mind. Your sister could do a lot worse."

"But she's so young. And so inexperienced."

"Whereas you have seen so much of the world," her companion said drily.

"I have my own beau, it would seem," Charlotte responded unenthusiastically. "What is your opinion of Lord Roxburgh?"

"He seems to have a good understanding, but I cannot like him. He is even more full of flowery speeches than your other admirers."

"I know. I find it hard to keep patience with them. It is amusing though, is it not, how many are paying court to me, even before I am truly back in circulation. I could wish their attentions were the result of genuine liking, but I suspect more than one has his eye on what was left to me of Ernest's fortune."

"You are wise to treat some of them with a degree of caution, I agree, but there will be many who will admire you for yourself alone, my dear, do not fear."

"Oh no, and as to that I am not in the least anxious to marry again. I shouldn't say it, I know, but you comprehend how it is with us. I can't tell you how good it feels to be my own mistress and no longer at the beck and call of Papa. Just as long as I can go about and meet people. It would in some part make up for what I am missing at Stapleton. I didn't realise at the time quite how much I enjoyed managing the estate. Far more entertaining than the needlework you tried so hard to teach me." Charlotte added, laughing, "For I had known the tenants all my life and could talk husbandry from dawn to dusk, knowing they didn't frown down upon me in private."

"You were much admired by them, I know, with far more knowledge and sensitivity to their needs than many a man in that position."

"As to that, I have certainly found it frustrating being cooped up for so long when I was used to such a different sort of life," Charlotte said wryly. "I don't quite know how to explain, Esther, but in spite of the constraints at Stapleton I had a freedom which I miss greatly. I've tried to hide it from Harriet, for my confinement necessitated hers as well because she would not hear of going about without me and she also must have been feeling restrained. And you too. I don't know what I would have done without the two of you to bear me company."

Charlotte looked at Esther, appealing for understanding, for it was not in her nature to complain or regret. More, she wanted her mentor's assurance that she perceived how she felt.

"You like your independence, I realise that, but there is time enough for you to reconsider your position. In the meantime, I have been thinking that soon you will be able to dance once again. What say you we have a tutor to come and remind you both of the steps you learned so long ago? You will be more at ease if you are familiar with the movements."

They had been conferring in low tones so as not to disturb the others in the room. Now Charlotte raised her voice a little. "What a good idea! Harriet, Esther is suggesting we have dancing lessons. You'd like that, wouldn't you?"

"Without a doubt," Harriet replied, looking up from her conversation with the seemingly ever-present Mr Peacock. "I would be nervous for certain to dance in public."

"But of course you must dance! And allow me if you would to be the first to lead you onto the floor," said Mr Peacock.

With dancing lessons, morning visits, walks about the square and trips, with the aim of replenishing their wardrobes, to the fashion houses so conveniently situated in Burlington Arcade, Jermyn Street and Bond Street, the young ladies had little time on their hands. Hours of sitting by the window with her needlework or the latest book from Hookham's Lending Library were for Charlotte a thing of the past, though she had always loved reading and escaping into a story had whiled away many a tedious hour.

It had been a long year.

CHAPTER FOUR

The next time Charlotte saw Gresham was the morning after his return to London. He had called a shade earlier than was fashionable, but Mr Peacock had already arrived before him.

"I came to see how the ladies are doing," Mr Peacock professed after greetings had been exchanged, though Gresham had sought no explanation.

"I am here on a similar errand. There is, however, another purpose to my visit, Lady Cranleigh," Gresham said, turning to his hostess, "perhaps you might step outside with me for a moment. There is something I would like you to see."

Charlotte was surprised. "In the street? Of course. Are the rest to come as well?" she asked, indicating the other three people in the room.

"I would prefer you came alone."

Charlotte felt disconcerted somehow. "Very well," she said, almost sweeping out of the room in front of him. Her attitude changed to one of amazement when the front door was opened by her footman. Standing patiently, her bridle being held by a groom, was a beautiful chestnut mare, her conformation exceptional, her breeding beyond question.

"What a beautiful horse! She is exquisite," Charlotte exclaimed, astonished and excited to see such a fine creature standing before her. "But why have you brought her to me?" she asked, her indignation forgotten in her genuine pleasure.

"She is a gift from the Duchess."

"Your wife?" Charlotte exclaimed, startled, the words from her lips before she could stop them. She felt foolish and a little piqued. "Ernest did not tell me you were married."

"Good heavens, no, I'm not," Gresham said, laughing aloud. "This is my mother's horse."

What an enigma he was. Charlotte felt embarrassed and was uncertain how to deal with the situation. "It's extremely kind of Her Grace, but I cannot possibly accept," she said more than a little wistfully.

"Do you always refuse well-meant gifts?"

"When they are as valuable as this one, yes, of course. In any case, why would the Duchess present me with a horse?"

"You would be doing her a favour. Sadly she is no longer able to ride. While it costs her a pang to part with Bess, she considers it unfair to keep her confined at Gresham Hall. 'She is far too noble a creature to be cooped up in her stable or put out to grass' is what she said to me."

"Bess, you say. It suits her. After the erstwhile queen, I presume."

Gresham bowed in acknowledgement of her swiftness of mind. "Assuredly. Would you like me to call the others to admire her?"

"No, please do not, for I still cannot accept her," Charlotte said with regret, though she could not prevent her hands from reaching up and stroking Bess's gleaming neck. The horse acknowledged what was her due by leaning towards the searching fingers.

"Think if you will, please. Bess has been my mother's pride and joy. She has had her from a filly and is no longer able to care for her as she would wish. We were discussing what was to become of her, and I mentioned that you had told me how much you missed riding. 'Is she competent enough to be trusted with Bess?' she asked me. 'I have no reason to believe otherwise' was my reply."

Naturally, Charlotte was flattered.

Gresham continued. "Her response was immediate. 'Beg her then, if she will, to do me the favour of taking Bess into her care and giving her the life I no longer can.' You will make her very happy, you know," he said. "Bess would be housed in your own stables and you would bear the cost of her keep. Otherwise, all that is required is that you exercise her regularly and love her as she deserves to be loved."

Charlotte wasn't proof against such temptation and said so. "And I shall write to thank the Duchess as soon as may be."

"Of course."

"And may we now fetch the others?" she asked, her excitement mounting by the moment.

"Certainly. I hope you can see now why I wanted you alone to join me out here."

"I cannot resist her! And yes, I understand, and I appreciate your thoughtfulness." And Charlotte did. His kindness too. She had not looked for so much sensibility in the man. Was there a generosity of spirit beneath his cool demeanour that she hadn't hitherto suspected?

"It would appear Mr Peacock is haunting your home," Gresham said with a smile as they returned to the house.

Charlotte laughed, the mood between them for once relaxed. "Yes, he would seem to have become something of a fixture."

Bess accepted the attention of her admirers with great good grace, not even flaring her nostrils as the group of five gathered close around her, for Esther too had come to worship. Charlotte stood at the mare's head whispering gently to her and Gresham watched in approval.

When their visitors had gone, Charlotte went at once to her room to search out her riding habit. Surely now there could be no objection to her venturing forth in such apparel. It was of a green woollen fabric which set off to perfection the colour of her hair.

She summoned Bella to help her try it on. The abigail looked in admiration, but Charlotte only laughed. She was less interested in the picture she made than in realising how well the green habit would look against Bess's gleaming chestnut coat. Reluctantly she removed the garment, together with the jockey bonnet which crowned the whole, but she determined to have the groom bring Bess around the very next morning so she could see how they fared together. She had no qualms about riding the mare around the crowded square. She'd already observed Bess's fine temperament.

Harriet and Esther stood at the top of the steps leading from the house, watching as Charlotte descended to where her groom was waiting with Bess. After murmuring to the mare and blowing gently into her nostrils, Charlotte placed her foot in the cup made by the groom's hands and mounted Bess as if riding were something she had done every day of her life, which until her marriage had almost been the case.

Settling into the saddle with her hand resting lightly on the pommel, Charlotte surveyed her surroundings. Prior to Ernest's accident she had been driven in one or other of the carriages, and indeed since, but this was a totally different experience. There was no frame surrounding her, no one else holding the reins, only the groom standing at her head, waiting. She was totally in control and anyone who knew her would recognise a kind of completeness as her body and that of the horse became almost as one.

Charlotte turned her head to smile at the ladies before commanding the groom, "Let her go, if you please."

The hand left the bridle and horse and rider set off at a gentle pace, using these first moments to get to know one another. Charlotte's hands were light, and the mare found no reason to champ at the bit.

Rider and horse returned to where the groom was waiting, and he led Bess off as Charlotte joined her companions in the morning room. Her eyes were sparkling with elation.

"I haven't seen you look so well since you left Stapleton," Esther remarked.

"Oh, Esther, it was marvellous! She is a challenge to be sure, but what a lady. I must write my thanks to the Duchess immediately, for I didn't do so yesterday. Now I hope I will be able to reassure her that Bess and I are compatible. How worried she must be. I know I should be in her place."

As the groom was removing the mare's tack, Charlotte was stepping out of her habit and into something more suitable, should visitors arrive. Arrive they did, but Charlotte didn't go down to greet them until she had written the promised letter. Only then did she join her guests, who appeared in the form of the ever-present Quentin Peacock and the impeccable figure of Viscount Roxburgh.

Charlotte was unsure how she felt about Roxburgh's visits, this his third. While he never stepped over the line, she felt somehow uncomfortable, as if he was hinting at an intimacy between them that she did not feel. On the other hand, he was entertaining and did not utter the insipid inanities for which she had so little time.

"Perhaps I am just not used to London ways," she had previously confided in Esther, raising the subject again because of her own uncertainties. "He assumes a manner I have never before encountered."

"He doesn't put you to the blush, but if it disconcerts you why not refuse his visits?"

"For that very reason. I have no just cause and I detest missish behaviours. He crosses no boundaries. His conversation is agreeable. There is just something I cannot quite be at ease with. It is such a comfort for me to have you here, Esther, to give me perspective. Thank heaven you agreed to join me when I left Hertfordshire."

"Well, if he asks you to stand up with him tomorrow, I can find reason to keep you by my side."

"No, for I have long promised Lord Roxburgh I will partner him and it would be grossly impolite if I were now to back down. In any case, it's nothing he has done. More an air of ownership. No, that is too strong an expression. I can't perfectly put it into words, but I cannot quite be relaxed in his company."

"Does Harriet say anything?"

"No, for she is so enraptured by Mr Peacock she sees nothing else."

"Are you worried by that connection?"

"No, not at all. He is a charming man. I just wish she had had more opportunity to meet others, but it seems she has tumbled head over heels in love with him. And he with her. It will do. He will make her happy."

"Why then do I feel you have some reservation?"

Charlotte could not answer her because in truth she did not like to admit how much, even though she would still have Esther to bear her company, she would miss her sister once she left to set up her own home. It seemed that day was coming far sooner than she had anticipated.

There was no way Charlotte would allow her apprehensiveness to become apparent the following evening, so it was with a smile that she permitted Roxburgh to take her hand and lead her to the floor, grateful only that the dance was not a waltz. In fact, the steps of the set ensured that they came together only for moments at a time and conversation was to say the least difficult.

"You are very proficient, Lady Cranleigh. It is evident you have had an excellent tutor."

It was impossible to reply as they moved apart, but at the next opportunity Charlotte said, "Why, thank you, sir. It is a pastime I enjoy very much."

Again they were separated.

"I too, though it is hard to converse in broken sentences," Roxburgh said ruefully.

"Let us then focus on the movements."

Roxburgh smiled his acknowledgement but, as he escorted Charlotte back to Esther's side, he asked if she might take a turn on the terrace with him, the evening being a mild one. For no reason she could explain, Charlotte felt a surge of apprehension and never had she been happier to see Gresham than when he appeared at her side and said, "I believe the next dance is mine, Lady Cranleigh." It was impossible not to feel the tension between the two men as Gresham led her away. She would have given much to know its cause.

For similar reasons as before, Charlotte was unable to converse sensibly with the Duke and she was grateful to have been given the opportunity to regain some of her earlier composure. When she was at last seated again, Esther said in a confidential tone, "You seemed less than comfortable when dancing with Roxburgh."

"Oh no! Did it show?" Charlotte was dismayed.

"No, I am certain no-one who does not know you well would have an inkling of your discomfiture."

Charlotte looked across at her sister, happily dancing with Mr Peacock, and smiled. "Harriet has no such apprehension, does she? I wish I could explain the way Roxburgh makes me feel. He adopts such a proprietorial air for which I am certain I have given him no cause."

"You sound uncertain."

"Only that I was perhaps a little friendlier than was wise on the first occasion we met."

"If he is a gentleman, he would not take advantage of such a lapse."

Charlotte could only agree.

CHAPTER FIVE

The elegant house in St. James's Square was coming to life. During her brief marriage to Ernest, Charlotte had not had time to stamp her own personality on a home she had not chosen but in the past months several changes had taken place.

Her own apartments had undergone a complete alteration. New furniture had been chosen to complement the transformation of the interior. It was this project that had in part kept her sane when having so much time on her hands. Harriet's bedroom, and Esther's too, had also undergone refurbishment.

The rest of the house remained the same, characterising as it did the taste she had so admired when seeing it for the first time. It had not though been much used. But now it was as if the whole place was emerging from beneath Holland covers.

"Oh do hurry, Charlotte, I need your advice."

"Yes, Harriet, I'll be with you as soon as I've changed my habit," Charlotte said, drawing off her gloves and laying them and her whip on a small table in the hall. "Bess delayed me, for she was nudging me for another titbit, convinced as she was that she'd earned extra today. Which indeed she had."

"Then I need not ask if you had a pleasant ride."

"No, indeed, Hyde Park was teeming with people but we were able to enjoy a swift canter along the row. However, several friends stopped us to pass the time of day and that, my dear impatient Harriet, is why I am so behind."

"How I envy you. I long to ride again."

"But why did you not say so before? How selfish of me, I'm so sorry." Charlotte was mortified. "We must set about finding a suitable mount for you, though it will be difficult to find a creature to compare to Bess."

"I have spoken to Mr Peacock about it. He assures me that we could do a lot worse than ask the Duke for advice, 'for he is the finest judge of horseflesh I know', he told me."

"I'd far rather have your company than that of my groom — it would be such fun! Like old times back at Stapleton! We must apply to His Grace the next time we see him."

"Will he be at tomorrow's ball, do you think?"

"I have no way of knowing. Only he once told me he prefers smaller gatherings where one may converse in comfort, which I found rather surprising. Presumably he must have to entertain a great deal, in his position."

"Tomorrow's event will most certainly not be a small gathering. I believe there will be above a hundred people there."

"Are you nervous?"

"No. Well, maybe a little, but very excited. Do hurry, Charlotte. I need you to help me choose which ribbons I should wear in my hair."

The following evening, after some excited comings and goings, the chosen cream ribbons had been threaded through Harriet's golden hair, a subtle and stylish adornment. Around her neck were clasped her mother's pearls, their colour exactly matching her muslin dress which was interwoven with ribbon of the identical hue to those in her hair. Ivory slippers completed the ensemble.

Charlotte looked at her fondly. "You'll do beautifully. You look calm and serene. Where oh where did my schoolroom sister go?"

"I feel much like that schoolroom sister, even if my appearance tells you otherwise. I have never before attended such a party. It's impossible not to feel a degree of apprehension."

"It's natural for you to do so, of course, but you have met many new people in the past few weeks and your manner has been all I could have wished," said Esther, who was trying to tuck in the wayward end of one ribbon that had escaped its mooring.

"It is only what you have taught me, dearest Esther. I pray I do not let you down."

"You won't, Harriet. And now that you have had some dancing lessons, you may feel confident of participating without embarrassment in the evening to come. Only remember that nothing could be more harmful than for you to be seen putting yourself forward in any way."

"She is more likely to hide behind your skirts as she did when we were children," Charlotte said, smiling fondly at her sister.

It seemed as though some of the attendants might be trampled underfoot, so crowded with carriages was Grosvenor Square, all rumbling to one house. But everything went smoothly except for one elderly lady, the hem of whose dress had snagged and torn on the step of her barouche as she struggled to get down.

"I thought you had a hold of your skirt, my dear," said her much berated spouse, who was deemed to bear responsibility for the incident.

"You had not my hand held firmly in yours. How could you have expected me to negotiate the steps of the barouche and hold my gown at the same time?"

He had no answer, for there was none. Unfortunately, he nonetheless attempted one and was left to follow meekly, muttering still, as his wife swept past him into the house. The Cranleigh party were witness to this exchange as theirs was the next carriage to draw up.

"Oh, poor man. Anyone could see it wasn't his fault," Charlotte remarked in sympathy.

"Just be sure the same doesn't happen to you. But lift your skirts carefully, as I have taught you. Not so high as to be deemed immodest."

"Yes, Esther," said her charges in unison, both fully aware of the anxiety she was feeling on their behalf. Her nerves always expressed themselves in an instruction to do this, or obliging them to do that. They smiled at each other and, fondly, at her.

"Go along, then. You first, Charlotte. The steps are down and I see an attendant waiting to guide you in. Yes, now you, Harriet," Esther said and followed them both into the glittering hallway of the magnificent townhouse.

They were led to a ballroom which had been built across the back of the house, the weather mild enough to allow the full length windows that led to the garden to be left open. Their host and hostess, close friends of Lady Stanford, greeted them as they entered and after a short exchange they moved on to make way for the persons coming in behind them.

There were gilt chairs lining the walls, interspersed with a sofa here and there, and some small tables. Above them the ceiling was hung with brilliant chandeliers which gave off so much light they almost dazzled the eye. Drapes hung on the walls and around the windows and there was a level of opulence which was exactly what the Earl and Countess of Flaxby had hoped to achieve.

All this Charlotte could see through such a dense crowd of people that it seemed they would be unable to make their way further into the room until all at once Gresham appeared beside them. She was very pleased to see him and more than a little grateful when he said, "Good evening, ladies. Allow me to lead you this way." He drew Charlotte's arm through his own, and gestured to Esther and Harriet to join them. "Mr Peacock is manfully guarding some seats which we have procured in anticipation of your arrival."

He guided them to one wall where Peacock was in the midst of an altercation with another gentleman who was trying to wrestle a chair from his hands.

"Dash it, I nearly had to call the fellow out," Peacock said as the unfortunate loser withdrew. "Couldn't seem to get him to understand that I'd engaged these for my own party. I hope I didn't presume, ladies. Such a crush, as I knew it would be, and we couldn't, Gresham and I, allow it to chance that there might be somewhere for you to sit."

No-one observing her would have seen anything remarkable in the glance Harriet gave Mr Peacock but there was gratitude there and, perhaps, a little hero worship as well. Charlotte reflected that if her sister's attachment to him endured, she would always be well-cared-for. He, and Gresham too, were the sort of men who could ever be relied upon to ensure one's comfort.

"It was kind of you both to think of us, and I for one am grateful," said Charlotte. "I fear otherwise my toes would have been trodden on many times."

"Did I not say I would look after you?" Gresham said. "It is my duty, after all."

That word duty again. Duty had caused Charlotte to manage her father's estate, duty had forced her into an unlooked-for marriage. Duty, it appeared, was what drove the Duke's interest in her. She would far rather friendship had been the motivation behind the gesture or, as it had been in Mr Peacock's case, adoration. Not that she wanted to be adored, but neither did she want these little attentions to be performed out of a sense of obligation.

Gresham seemed to sense her slight withdrawal. "Not that I deem it anything but a pleasure and a privilege. It is an honour, Lady Cranleigh, to do what I can to help."

"Look, they are forming up in the centre," Peacock remarked as people surged towards the walls to make room, thus causing an even greater crush. "May I have the honour, Miss Willoughby?"

"I believe I am promised to you, sir. Thank you, I should be delighted."

"I would be happy if I could lead you in every dance," her swain whispered ardently to Harriet as he led her to the floor. She flushed becomingly as they took their places.

Charlotte's hand was just being solicited for by Gresham when they were cut in upon by Lord Roxburgh.

"You must wait in line, Your Grace, for I think you will find I have a prior claim on Lady Cranleigh for this dance."

Roxburgh put out his arm to Charlotte in a somewhat demanding way, but he was correct. The dance had long been promised to Roxburgh and she had no choice but to take the proffered hand. She disliked his attitude — it was too proprietorial — nor was she comfortable with the touch of his fingers as they took hers. What she liked even less was the fire that flared up in Gresham's eyes and the look of animosity that went with it.

Always conscious of Lord Roxburgh's somewhat overly familiar behaviour, Charlotte fancied on this occasion that she could feel a menace emanating from within the man who to all outward appearances was as charming as ever. He smiled, he spoke not a word inappropriately, but did his fingers linger on hers for longer than was customary or acceptable?

Her first dance of the evening, something she had been for so long looking forward to, became a disappointment and she was never more grateful than when it finished and he led her back to Esther and, after a few words of conversation, withdrew. Harriet and Mr Peacock had not yet returned from the floor, and Gresham was nowhere to be seen.

"You look disturbed, Charlotte. Is it Roxburgh?"

"Yes, Esther, though I am sorry it shows so plainly. I must strive to control my features."

"No-one who did not know you would realise, but there is a glitter in your eyes that has nothing to do with the reflection from the chandeliers."

"He did nothing wrong. Nothing I could say was improper other than that perhaps he held my hand a little longer than convention dictates. But that could just be me, of course. I have so little experience of these things."

"I feel sure you are right, Charlotte. A girl knows these things instinctively. If he approaches you again, you will excuse yourself from dancing with him."

"But how can I do that without also declining to dance with others? And I am promised to him later in the evening. For a waltz of all things. Just the thought of his arms about me is repugnant."

"You will not be forced if it is against your wishes. And we will refuse him if he comes again to the house."

"How can we, Esther? He is accepted everywhere, as far as I know."

"I will not have you made uncomfortable," Esther said with considerable emphasis. "You are Lady Cranleigh and you have the right to receive or deny the attentions of anyone. Too much of your life already has been spent in complying with the wishes of others."

Charlotte began to calm down under Esther's assurances but, feeling flushed, she unfurled her fan and waved it in front of her face.

Gresham approached a few moments later and smiled in sympathy, remarking that it was indeed a sad crush. "Perhaps you would enjoy a stroll on the terrace? I believe it is quite a mild evening. Indeed I know it, for I have just returned from there."

"Yes, do take her, Your Grace, for it will do her good to get a little fresh air."

"You must think me a poor creature," said Charlotte.

"Not at all," Gresham replied. "Recall I have seen you ride in the park. Nobody who understands horses so well could ever in my opinion be regarded in that light."

"It is very hot inside."

"Which is why I have always preferred parties where there are fewer people. How anyone is supposed to be able to conduct an intelligent conversation in that heat, with all that noise, I have never understood."

"It seems not to have affected my sister."

"Your sister is a beautiful young woman who is enjoying her first magnificent outing. It is not to be thought she would regard a slight rise in temperature."

"Slight?"

"Perhaps a little more than slight."

They walked in silence for a few minutes, and little by little Charlotte regained her composure. They stepped from the terrace into the garden and found a stone bench where, after he had checked that it was not damp, Gresham suggested she sit down. They were in full sight of the open windows, so there was no question of impropriety.

"Speaking of Harriet…" Charlotte began.

"Were we?"

"Yes. You mentioned once before that your friend is frequently to be seen in her company, but I would value your opinion should you choose to give it."

"You wish me to tell you if I think Quentin is seriously considering offering for Miss Willoughby? Yes, I do. We have been friends for a long time, and I have never seen him so much as glance at another woman above three times."

"It seems to me he can do nothing but glance at Harriet. It is my dearest wish that she be happily settled, but it seems all to have happened so quickly. There can be no doubt as to her feelings for him either, but would it be a good match?"

Gresham looked at Charlotte steadily. "You cannot expect me to discuss Mr Peacock's private affairs with you, surely? His family, you may be assured, is an ancient and noble one, though he doesn't carry a title. That has gone to his older brother. For the rest, it is not for me to say."

Charlotte felt that he was deliberately misunderstanding her. Did he believe her to be seeking a wealthy match for her sister following her own? "No, of course I would not wish you to discuss personal circumstances. That isn't what I meant at all. It's just, well, that day you brought Bess to me you remarked about him haunting my home. I wondered if there was anything behind your question that I ought to know about."

Gresham burst out laughing. "No, dear lady —" Charlotte was not sure whether she liked this term of address — "there is nothing you need to know about Quentin Peacock that won't have been immediately obvious if you have ever held any conversation with him. A nicer man you could not hope to find and one whose friendship I value immensely. It was merely that, forgive me if I speak out of turn, I imagined you would have wanted your sister to have been out in society a little longer before forming an attachment."

"Exactly!" she said with feeling. "I'm so glad you understand my concern. But it seems the die is cast."

"Ah, you are a gamester. Do you play cards as well?"

"Do not mock me, sir, and yes, I do like to play occasionally."

"Don't play with Roxburgh."

The interjection was sudden and surprised Charlotte.

"It is not for you to dictate with whom I play," she retorted, more than a little piqued, though in truth she would not have wished to engage in a game with Roxburgh.

"My apologies, Lady Cranleigh. I spoke out of turn. Are you cool enough now? Would you like to return to the ballroom?"

Charlotte rose as Gresham did, reflecting that every time they came towards understanding each other, something seemed to occur to make her feel uneasy again.

After Charlotte had returned indoors with Gresham, Cosmo Fortescue, whom she had met on that first walk with Gresham and Mr Peacock, had taken her down to supper and proved to be an entertaining companion. She had been solicited to dance several times, but all the while she was dreading the moment when Lord Roxburgh would claim her for the waltz.

Gresham disappeared, to one of the card rooms she discovered later, and she tried not to feel abandoned. She had no claim on his protection, after all, in spite of his assertions to the contrary. However, their earlier conversation had been enjoyable until his unlooked-for comment about playing cards with Roxburgh, and there was no denying her relief when he appeared again in the ballroom just moments before the waltz was struck up.

Roxburgh approached and she went with him to the floor, reflecting that she knew what Daniel must have felt when entering the lion's den. But she determined not let her apprehension show. At that moment, she caught Gresham's eye, and although he clearly registered that she was on Roxburgh's arm, he smiled at her reassuringly, which eased the sting of his earlier remark.

Charlotte did stiffen for a moment at the start when Roxburgh's arm encircled her waist, but she had, under Mr Talbot's instruction, become used to being held thus and was able to bear it with composure. She managed to remember her steps and even smiled inwardly as she recalled Esther's remarks about concentration and facial expression.

As Lord Roxburgh returned her to Esther's side, he begged leave to come and visit her again soon. Short of being rude, Charlotte could think of nothing to deter him and merely said coolly, "We shall be delighted, sir," afterward turning to Esther and whispering, "What else could I say?"

"Nothing, my dear, and even if you had I doubt it would have deterred him. It's easy to see that he is hoping to win you, Charlotte."

"Not me, but my fortune or, rather, Ernest's fortune. There is something cold and calculating about the man, despite his polished exterior."

"I cannot but agree with you. Well, you must keep him at an arm's length and we must ensure he is never left alone with you."

Thereafter the evening improved for Charlotte, for she could at last relax. Gresham, at one time sitting by her side, spoke quietly so none could hear. "I need not ask you if you are pleased with Bess. I have seen you riding in the park on several occasions. You look almost resentful when called to rein in and converse with pedestrians or other riders."

"Oh dear, and I am always at such pains to ensure it doesn't show," Charlotte said ruefully. However, she could not help but feel pleased at the implied compliment.

"By the by, Lady Cranleigh, my mother is hoping to pay one of her very rare visits to town soon and has expressed the hope that she might meet you. You will not, I am sure, be offended when I say I suspect it is because she wishes to satisfy herself that all is well with Bess."

"No, not at all," she replied, laughing in appreciation. "I am sure I would feel exactly the same. I should be delighted to meet Her Grace. Does she come soon?"

"In a few weeks. She would choose to travel when the weather is warmer and kinder to her bones. That it is an ordeal for her, I have no doubt, but she would not forego her annual visit to the capital under any but the most extreme circumstances. She says it sets her up for the rest of the year."

"Does she miss it so, the life in London?"

"I think not, for she was always used to spend the greater part of the year at Gresham Hall, even when my father was in town. Her horses were everything to her, and if she had them nothing else mattered."

"Not even her son?" Charlotte said teasingly.

"I came a close second," he replied with a laugh. "Fortunately I had a similar interest, even when growing up, so I never had cause to feel abandoned or neglected because she would nearly always take me with her."

"So it was a passion with you even as a boy?"

"Without a doubt. In fact, I met a lad recently who reminded me…" He left the sentence unfinished.

Instinctively realising that he had thought better of confiding in her, Charlotte looked questioningly at him, but Gresham turned the subject and soon rose to relinquish his seat to Mr Peacock, who obviously wanted to engage her in conversation.

"I trust you are having a pleasant evening, Lady Cranleigh."

"Indeed I am. It has been so long since I had the opportunity of engaging with so many people."

"Miss Willoughby seems also to be enjoying herself," Peacock replied, turning the talk to where he wished it to be.

Charlotte was amused, rather than offended by his single-mindedness but she was glad to have the opportunity to talk with him. She had at first thought him a trifle old for Harriet, since he was close to Gresham in age, but his influence upon her had only been beneficial and she had been brought to thinking they might do very well together.

"I had a wonderful time!" Harriet exclaimed, as she settled herself back against the cushions of the carriage. "It was everything I had hoped it would be and more."

"I think it went very well, my dear," Esther replied. "I was pleased that you behaved so prettily and didn't spend the evening hanging upon Mr Peacock's sleeve."

"Esther, I would never … I hope I would never spend the evening hanging on any gentleman's sleeve."

"She is teasing you, Harriet," Charlotte said, smiling fondly at her sister. "We are aware that you hold him in very high regard. How could we not be?"

Harriet didn't deny it. Instead she stammered, "Would you … if he … if I…?"

"Don't put yourself into a taking. We have all grown fond of Mr Peacock, have we not, Esther? It is only that you have known him barely a few weeks, and I had so hoped you would have the opportunity of enjoying your first season unencumbered."

"Unencumbered!"

Charlotte took her sister's hand. "No, not that of course, but free at least to broaden your horizons before making such a commitment. However, it is of little use to talk so when one would have to be a fool not to see that your affections are already engaged. Has he spoken to you of this?"

"He said he hoped that he had a chance with me. That he would wait until I had been out for a while. That I should have some space to think. But I don't need to think. Charlotte. Esther. I love him." Despite her youth, Harriet spoke with the calm certainty of someone who knew her own mind.

"Then I couldn't be happier for you. It is my dearest wish that you marry for love."

CHAPTER SIX

Charlotte returned from her ride the next day to find an unexpected visitor.

"Papa! I had no notion you were in town."

"No, how could you when I am only just returned from Warwickshire. It will be months before the hunting season is upon us and things are sadly flat at the moment. So I took a fancy to see how my girls were getting along, and your man was happy enough to allow me to wait when I told him who I was."

Charlotte chose to ignore the doubtful compliment, saying instead, "Harriet is not yet returned from her walk, I believe. She will be glad to see you, I'm sure."

It was unlikely that this would be the case but his daughter gave Sir Archibald due deference, at the same time wondering what was the real reason for his visit.

"May I offer you some refreshment?"

"That would be most welcome, thank you."

Charlotte rang the bell and it seemed from the way he lounged in the chair that her father's visit would be of some duration. The tray was brought in at the same time as Harriet and Esther entered the room, and only good manners prevented the older lady from retreating immediately. She had no affection whatever for her charges' father, and no-one was more aware than she of how sadly he had neglected them in earlier years. She had reason to suspect his peccadillos began even before the demise of his wife. And not for the world would she have mentioned to Charlotte and Harriet that he had behaved inappropriately towards her on more than one occasion. Only her affection, firstly for her aunt and then for the girls, had prevented her packing her bags and leaving many years ago, and it now prevented her from making an abrupt exit from the room. She didn't, however, feel obliged to stay for long and excused herself after the conventional greetings had taken place. Charlotte followed her out, saying she needed to change out of her riding habit, and Harriet was left alone with her father.

"London obviously suits you, my girl. You're looking in fine form."

"Indeed, our lives have changed since Charlotte's period of mourning came to an end. It is so nice to be able to go out again."

"Well, it has all worked out for the best, it seems. No doubt you will be looking for a husband of your own."

Harriet could not like this turn of conversation, as if what her sister had been through was nothing and she was merely looking to establish herself in society. "We have barely begun to go about, Papa. It is far too soon to be thinking about the future."

She was of course thinking of precisely that, but it certainly wasn't something she was going to share with her father. Conversation became a little desultory and she was at a loss as to what to say next when her sister returned.

Charlotte could see immediately from the pleading look Harriet sent her that she had been struggling. In her usual calm manner she resolved the situation by saying to their father, "You will forgive us, I am sure, but we have promised to visit some friends. Thank you for calling upon us. Do you stay long in town?"

She did not sit down and, as Harriet rose, Sir Archibald had no choice but to take his leave, telling them that he wasn't sure what would be the duration of his visit and that he was staying at Fenton's Hotel should they wish to contact him. He would come and see them again before leaving town.

"What a fib, Charlotte," Harriet said when Sir Archibald had left. "Visiting friends indeed."

"No such thing. I didn't say when we would be visiting them. We're bound to visit someone soon," Charlotte replied, the green flecks flashing in her eyes as they always did when she was amused.

"But I'm so glad he's gone. I hardly knew what to say to Papa and didn't even ask how things were at Stapleton. Do you think he noticed?"

"I'm fairly sure he didn't. He seemed a little apart from us. Even more so than usual. I think he was taken up with his own affairs and merely made this call out of a sense of duty."

"Is it wrong to feel as I do, Charlotte? I cannot hold him in affection."

"No, it's not wrong. He has done nothing to earn our affection. We will always, I hope, treat him with the respect that is owed to a parent, but beyond that his life need not touch ours."

Charlotte heard nothing of her father for the next few days. Following the ball, the number of visitors to St James's Square increased considerably and she found it hard indeed to make time to take Bess out every day. Conscious of her responsibility to such a noble animal she wasn't prepared to forego the obligation, such was their combined pleasure in the activity. Seeing her dilemma, Esther reassured her that she would chaperone Harriet.

People came in equal numbers to see the sisters, men and women alike. Popular though Harriet was, Charlotte was amused to find that several gentlemen callers admired her and, finding the Countess absent, began themselves to ride in the Park in the hope of accosting her. While she was flattered, she was no fool, and easily identified the fortune hunters. But she was not looking to marry again. She assumed that after her sister's inevitable marriage she would live in harmony with Esther, enjoying all the pleasures of a social life and neither needing nor wanting a husband. She considered herself incapable of feeling the affection she perceived between Harriet and Mr Peacock.

Cosmo Fortescue proved to be an amiable companion and of all Charlotte's visitors, the gentleman with whom she most felt an affinity. She judged he had no pretensions to her hand, merely enjoying the company of what he referred to as a sensible woman — "For you must know, Lady Cranleigh, that there are many who can talk only of the latest fashion or the last ball they attended."

Much of their conversation was of their mutual love of horses but Fortescue, when he discovered the range of Charlotte's knowledge regarding the management of a country estate, was most impressed and urged her to tell him more of her life at Stapleton. While not trying to show herself in an exceptional light, it was evident from what she said that there could be no doubting her capabilities and his admiration for her, already strong, increased greatly.

It was during one of his visits that Lord Roxburgh came too. His attendance was not of long duration, but Fortescue remarked when he had gone, "I fear you were not quite pleased to see Roxburgh. I beg you would call upon me if he importunes you in any way. I will be only too pleased to send him on his way."

"It is kind of you indeed, Cosmo," Charlotte said, for they had quickly become close friends and were on first name terms, "but he doesn't step out of line. It's just that I cannot feel quite composed when he is about."

"I know what you mean. One sees him everywhere, but I do not like the fellow. Bad *ton*, if you ask me, though he hides it well."

It was only too evident from the inclination of her head that Charlotte agreed with him.

The Duke of Gresham had called a few days after the ball. As he was so obviously dressed for riding Charlotte did not anticipate his visit would be a long one, but he surprised her.

"My groom walks my horse outside. I was hoping I had timed my visit correctly and that you might be preparing even now to ride Bess. I see you are indeed wearing your habit. Would you allow me to join you?"

"You wish, I apprehend, to see if you can reassure your mother that I am competent," she said teasingly.

"No such thing. I have no such anxieties. I have told you already that I have observed you in the park. But it would give me pleasure to ride with you."

Charlotte was not proof against this sort of flattery and was a little disturbed to realise how much the comment meant to her, coming from a man whose prowess in the saddle was known to all.

Bess was brought round to the front of the house in a few minutes. They set off together and, after a brisk canter in the park which satisfied both riders and horses alike, they walked together in perfect harmony, no subject causing any dissention between them. The Duke asked if she had enjoyed the ball, but neither mentioned Lord Roxburgh. Charlotte confided in him that the increase in morning callers would, had she let it, have interfered with her attention to the beautiful chestnut whose neck she stroked even as she spoke of her. "For you must know they are not all come to see Harriet," she said demurely, lowering her eyelashes.

"I would have been surprised had that been the case," he responded.

"I wonder if I might beg the favour of your advice, your Grace?" Charlotte said. "It concerns finding a horse, and seeing your beautiful Sable I feel sure you are the right person to ask."

"There can be no doubt you are delighted with Bess. Is it that you wish me to help you in buying some horses for your carriage?"

"No, indeed, thank you. The Earl's stable is still complete. The only gelding we parted with was Rufus, for he was unsuitable for me to ride. But Harriet has expressed a desire to ride again, and I would love her to share the pleasure that means so much to both of us. We have nothing appropriate for her and I was hoping you might consent to look out for something on our behalf."

"Are we talking about a gentle lady's mount?"

Charlotte smiled at the thought, picturing her sister careering all over the countryside when back at Stapleton. "Don't even suggest such a thing, and certainly not to Harriet!" she said laughingly. "She was thrown so many times as a child and always blamed herself for being cow-handed. She would climb back up again immediately. No, something with a bit of spirit would suit her admirably if we knew where to look."

"A bit of a hoyden, is she?" he said, sounding amused.

"Not at all," she replied, bridling slightly on her sister's behalf. "Just a girl who was used to enjoying country pursuits in a safe environment."

"Forgive me, I was not levelling a criticism. It's an interesting insight into the character of a young lady who is always so prettily behaved."

Charlotte recalled the conversation not long ago when Harriet had expressed a desire to be striding across fields with the wind in her hair, and laughed again. "Esther has done her work well, but I believe Harriet to be a country girl at heart."

"And you? Are you also a country girl?"

It wasn't something Charlotte had considered before, but though she had always, when forbidden to do so, had a strong desire to visit town, she realised that she missed the quietness and serenity of her childhood home. "I hadn't thought about it much, but I believe I enjoy living both in the metropolis with all its noise and excitement and also the rural tranquillity that I was used to before my marriage."

"You are in the fortunate position of being able to enjoy both, unless anything particular keeps you in London?"

"No, and in fact we plan when the season ends to visit Bath or perhaps Brighton. We might of course return to Stapleton for a while, for it is still Harriet's home, but we aren't sure when our father will be there or even if it will be convenient. We have not yet made a firm decision." She said nothing of their distaste for Sir Archibald's company.

Charlotte was enjoying London immensely. She had been used to an active and full life at Stapleton. She occasionally reflected that the Duke had said she was in a position to enjoy the best of both worlds, but this wasn't quite true. As spring turned into summer, the city became hotter and a little oppressive. While Bath or Brighton would make a change, they were still towns. She had visited neither but was prepared, from what she had been told, to believe each held merit. But it would be impossible for her to walk as energetically as she was accustomed to at Stapleton in either the seaside resort or the genteel spa. That she could only do somewhere in the country and out of sight of a critical world.

In her heart of hearts, Charlotte felt Stapleton was lost to her. While Harriet perhaps still regarded it as her real home, Charlotte could not. She didn't know how much time her father spent there and wondered whether she would resent the changes made since Ernest had rescued her parent from his difficulties. It would seem strange to be there and no longer responsible for its management. Her late husband's country seat had passed to the Duke, so there was now no tranquil retreat to which she felt she could retire. However, if it was Harriet's wish to go to their childhood home she would accompany her, though she dreaded the thought of returning as a visitor, and she sensed also that Esther would be reluctant to return.

"We must again consider, must we not, where we will spend the summer," Charlotte said to Harriet and Esther one afternoon, following a dawdling walk in particularly sultry weather. Her sister's response was lukewarm.

"I had rather stay in London, I believe. We have made so many friends I should be sad to leave them now."

Charlotte thought she understood exactly the reason for Harriet's remark, but it was left to Esther to ask, "What are Mr Peacock's plans, do you know?"

Harriet had the grace to blush but said she rather thought he meant to remain in the capital for a while before visiting his brother and family in the country. She dreaded the loss of his company, though she omitted to say this aloud. Still determined to do the right thing by her, Mr Peacock had not approached her father and though she could not but be reassured when they were together, which was often, she sometimes had misgivings. Alone in her room at night, for example, when she wondered if so sophisticated a man who had avoided matrimony thus far would not soon tire of an inexperienced young girl. She was not one who believed that her absence would increase his fondness for her, and determined to remain as close to him as she could for as long as she could.

Charlotte, not aware of her sister's insecurity, felt the time was fast approaching when a decision must be made. "I'm sure many of those friends you speak of will be leaving town before long. I believe Brighton to be a most superior place and the Prince Regent's home something out of the ordinary. Would you like me to look into hiring a house there for the summer?"

"I don't know."

This lacklustre response left Charlotte at a loss to know what to say next. Putting aside her own qualms, she said, "We could return to Stapleton if you would like. Imagine striding around in the open, your hair flying in the wind. How liberating that would feel. What do you think?"

"I don't know. You don't understand!" Harriet said, and flung out of the room.

Raising her eyebrows, Charlotte had to acknowledge to Esther that her sister was right, she didn't understand. It is true she was feeling weary and a little forlorn herself, but she put that down to the effects of the weather. "And if that's what being in love makes you feel like, I can only be grateful that I am now established and can enjoy the company of friends without all the unease that seems to go with being so attached to another."

Charlotte next saw Gresham at Almack's a week or so after their ride in the park. It was her first visit to those hallowed rooms, and both she and Harriet were slightly apprehensive.

"You have only to conduct yourself as usual and all will be well," Esther had assured them.

"But I have heard of people being ostracised following some perceived indiscretion," Harriet replied.

"Which neither of you is likely to commit. The Countess of Jersey has been kind enough to bestow vouchers upon you, and will hopefully present some gentleman to you for the waltz. You have but to behave in your accustomed way."

It was Cosmo Fortescue who had engaged to escort the ladies to King Street and who succeeded in his usual easy-going way to put them at their ease. "I trust you have dined well. The refreshments are unremarkable, though I must insist you didn't hear that from me."

"Indeed that rumour had already reached us," Charlotte laughed, "though I believe lemonade and tea are available, and I am partial to tea."

"Then you will do well. Ah, here we are. Allow me to help you down."

Charlotte glanced up briefly at the arched windows on the first floor before taking her friend's arm and entering that exclusive establishment. It was already crowded inside but not so much to render her unable to take in a large balcony, supported by pillars, which accommodated several persons who looked out onto the spacious hall. Large chandeliers hung from the ceiling and no expense had been spared in the adornment of the interior. Yet they had been guests in more splendid ballrooms.

"It's not nearly as impressive as I thought it would be, don't you agree, Charlotte?" Harriet asked her. "I feel much more composed now we are actually here."

"Yes, but so necessary to one's social standing to be admitted that it is, I believe, built up out of all proportion. Though we must still be grateful to Lady Jersey for granting us access. And for heaven's sake, don't criticise it to her or we shall be blackballed!" said Charlotte, and they stifled guilty giggles as they moved towards the Patronesses.

Gresham arrived about an hour later and approached Charlotte when she was, for a moment, sitting alone. He smiled at the rather rueful expression on her face as she watched her sister dancing with Mr Peacock.

"You do not approve?"

"Oh no, not that, for they deal so well together, don't they? It's only that I am increasingly feeling the need to get away from London for a while. Esther too. But it would be selfish, would it not, to part two people who so obviously want to be together."

"Do you always think of others before yourself, Lady Cranleigh?"

Charlotte was surprised by the question, because to her it was obvious that she should consider the interests of those whom she held in affection. "Far from it, or I wouldn't leave my sister each day to ride when she is still unable to join me," she replied, smiling. "However, your friend's attentions are so marked now, his presence ever felt, that I have no doubt I am not missed."

"I wished to speak to you on that very subject. I have not as yet been able to locate what I might consider a suitable mount for Miss Willoughby. However, I am shortly going to Gresham Hall to escort my mother back to London. There is a gelding in my stable that could fit the bill very nicely. Would it suit you for me to bring him back with me?"

"But I couldn't take one of your horses!"

"Of course not," he replied, his tone a trifle short. "Naturally I would set a reasonable price on him."

She bit her lip. She had been guilty of a presumption, though he had after all, she thought resentfully, given her his mother's horse. How was she to know that this new offer was different in nature? Mortified, she said stiffly, "In that case, I should be very much obliged to you."

He bowed. "Then I shall see you on my return. My mother, by the way, sends her regards and tells me she is greatly looking forward to meeting you, *and* to seeing Bess again."

Reflecting a few days later, Charlotte had to acknowledge that she missed her occasional encounters with Gresham. Trying to explain this feeling to herself, she wondered whether it was because he inspired trust as Papa never had. No, that was ridiculous. He was far too young to be regarded as a father figure. It was rather that he was a solid presence on whose judgement she felt she could rely, and she was human enough to be aware it was an honour to be singled out by him.

There were many times when she had seen a disdainful expression on his face, and he had a manner of distancing himself from people when he chose. On those occasions, she could not like him as well and attributed it to his being an indulged only child, very conscious of his rank. To her, though, he was kind, only once or twice causing her to feel like a foolish and impertinent child. It wasn't what she had been used to. Wise beyond her years, life had taught her to stand on her own feet and relish her independence. *And I must maintain that independence, for who can tell when he may choose to withdraw his support?* she told herself sternly.

CHAPTER SEVEN

Charlotte was feeling bored and lethargic, which she continued to blame on the weather. However, on meeting Cosmo Fortescue in the park one morning, she found her spirits lifting. His horse fell in beside hers and they walked at a pace which made for easy conversation.

"How on earth do you remain so cool, Cosmo? I fear you will consider me unladylike if I confess to finding this weather very trying."

"You look, as ever, immaculate, if I may be permitted to say so."

"Then my looks belie what I feel. Do you not feel this oppression in the air?"

"We must all do so. It is short notice, I know, but perhaps if you are free you might enjoy a drive out of town tomorrow afternoon. A breath of the country might help to restore you."

"What a lovely idea. I should be delighted."

"Then I shall bring a picnic and invite your sister and cousin also."

"Thank you. Just the thought of seeing fields and grass and I am feeling better already."

In the end it was a party of six who ventured out the next day. Mr Peacock was found to be in St James's Square when Cosmo escorted Charlotte to her door and the invitation was extended to him and also to a Mr George Harvey, who had taken of late to visiting the house. To the amusement of both sisters, the object of his attention was Esther, and for the first time in all the years they had known her she was found to blush whenever that gentleman's name was mentioned.

"You don't think there's a match in the air, do you?" Harriet had asked Charlotte, obviously incredulous. "I never thought to see Esther married!"

"Nor I, but there is no doubt that there is a new spring in her step. We have been so used to regarding her as a mother figure, have we not, that it has never occurred to us she might wish for a husband of her own."

"Well, she certainly never gave us any cause to think so. But what do we know about George Harvey? I would not wish her to fall in love with a man who was unable to care for her as we would wish."

Charlotte laughed out loud. "What a reversal of roles this is! For so long Esther has been our mentor and guide and now we are behaving like the mother hen who fusses over her chicks. Well, if he is to come with us on this picnic, we will be better able to observe him. I like him, though. He seems to give Esther every attention without behaving in any way improperly. It would seem that Esther likes him too. Who would have imagined a situation like this a year or so ago?"

"Is she not past the age of hoping for marriage?"

"I doubt any woman is ever past hope, Harriet."

Privately, from the perspective of her nineteen years, Harriet considered Esther far too old to be considering such a step, but that she was considering it seemed to be the case.

The years had treated Esther well and, with an assured bearing and an impeccable taste in attire, she was always immaculately turned out, and as such was gratified to be receiving almost as much attention as her juniors. George Harvey was not her sole suitor, but he was the only one who had aroused her interest. He was a man with a serious turn of mind, of a similar age to her own, but he possessed a sense of humour which frequently came to the fore. Esther felt entirely at ease with him and, when in his company, had no regret for her crumbling defences. It was therefore with the anticipation of a day of unalloyed pleasure that each member of the group left the oppression of London behind and headed out into the country.

Cosmo had done his work well. He had ordered a picnic which would have satisfied twice their number, and rugs had been provided so the ladies should not stain their delicate frocks on the grass. Though it hadn't rained for some time, the benefit of the fresher country air was felt by all. The atmosphere in the capital was more than usually crushing for the time of year, and, while the wealthier classes were making plans to escape, it was still early in the season yet for them to be abandoning town for country.

"I feel like a dowager looking after her charges," Charlotte confided in Cosmo as first Harriet and Quentin, then Esther and George, distanced themselves by just a few feet from the rest so they could enjoy some private conversation.

"Would it be all right if Mr Peacock and I ventured in the direction of that small copse, Charlotte? The trees are throwing some shade and it might be a little cooler there."

"Of course. Don't go too far, though. It will be time soon to be turning back."

The young couple went off happily, and while the other two didn't abandon them it was evident they would have preferred to be alone.

"Mr Fortescue desires to show me the finer points of his horses, if you will excuse us for a while," Charlotte said to her cousin. She was rewarded with a warm look which indicated just how strong Esther's feelings were for Mr Harvey.

It seemed to Charlotte that it would not be long before both her cousin and her sister were setting up their own homes. Independent though she was, she could not help worrying what her own future might hold, for she had no close friend suitable to bear her company if both Harriet and Esther left. She could not live alone and, while she turned her mind to find a solution, it was not that which exercised her so much as the sense of loneliness she seemed to be feeling so often of late. This came to her most strongly when she retired to bed and many a night had been spent with little sleep. Nevertheless, she couldn't have been happier for her family and felt that after a somewhat confined mode of living, both Harriet and Esther were in a way to establishing themselves in just such a manner as they would wish. Charlotte's sense of loneliness, though, remained.

"I hope you don't mind, Cosmo. Esther and Mr Harvey were so obviously craving some time alone." Charlotte was stroking the neck of one of the horses and looked up when there was no response, wondering at her friend's silence. She found him looking at her somewhat quizzically and smiled, a question in her eyes.

"You are quite unconscious, are you not, of the picture you present? There is a calmness and beauty about you that shines in all you do. Had you not suggested we look at the horses, I would myself have found some excuse to separate you from our companions."

The smile turned to a look of concern. Charlotte had not seen this coming. She had long regarded Mr Fortescue as a trusted friend, not considering for a moment that he had pretensions to her hand, but there could be no doubting the implication of his last words. He was quick to read her expression.

"You had no perception, had you, that I have fallen deeply in love with you. That I have your friendship you have made clear. If I could have your love, nothing would give me greater joy than to make you my wife."

He stepped towards her but she put up her hand, distressed to know that she was about to give pain to someone she was fond of.

"Cosmo, I am fully conscious of the honour you do me, but I have never regarded you in the light of suitor. Your friendship I value more than I can say. I have become so used to being able in your company to abandon those restrictions which convention dictates we must adopt and enjoying the pleasure of being myself."

"And I hope it will always be so."

"If I may be frank with you, I have not, since Ernest's passing, given any thought to marrying again. It seems far too soon to be contemplating such a thing," Charlotte said, by now quite agitated at this unexpected turn of events. Doubtless an alliance with Cosmo would be a solution to her problem, and certainly she would be comfortable with him, but never again would Charlotte marry where she did not love.

"Say no more. I have spoken too hastily. Please do not distress yourself. I hope that in time your feelings towards me will grow warmer. Meanwhile I shall continue, if you will permit me, to be your friend."

"My feelings for you, Cosmo, are warm indeed, but they are not those of a woman in love. Believe me, I do not look to marry again."

"Then let us pretend, if we may, that this conversation did not take place. You have been, as always, open and honest with me and I would not for the world make you feel embarrassed.

Trust that I will not further put you to the blush. I sincerely wish we might continue as before."

"I too, dear Cosmo, for I value your friendship very dearly."

Unnoticed by anyone, the sky had darkened and all at once the heavens opened. They rushed to take shelter in the copse which Harriet and Quentin had occupied, but the rain was fierce indeed and none was dressed for inclement weather. It wasn't long before they were all soaked through, so they abandoned their inadequate shelter and set out for home. The rain which followed them didn't cease in its ferocity and it was six very wet and bedraggled people who arrived back in St James's Square. Cosmo escorted the ladies into the house and then volunteered to drive the rest of the party to their respective homes.

When the gentlemen called the next day, they were distressed to find that Esther had taken a severe chill and was confined to her chamber. Cosmo was mortified, taking the responsibility upon himself. "For it was I who invited her and must take the blame for not taking proper care."

"You no more than the rest of us could have anticipated such a dramatic change in the weather, Cosmo," Charlotte assured him. "Until the rain began, we were all of us having a lovely time and I am convinced Esther would be the first to scold you for censuring yourself."

He could not see it thus and asked Charlotte to carry his deepest regrets to her cousin. Their conversation of the previous day was not referred to but it was something Charlotte had spent much of the night thinking about.

"At least the storm has cleared the air and London is not now as intolerable as it was," she said lightly.

But Esther became increasingly ill. A fever took hold and it was obvious from the doctor's demeanour that he had grave misgivings about her condition.

"There is little you can do for her until the fever passes. Administer the paregoric draught which I shall have sent around. She may find it soothing. Perhaps you have a screen you can put up to shelter her from the light as I see the sun comes straight through that window there. We must be grateful that the humidity has lessened. I will visit again tomorrow. Good day."

Charlotte found very little to be grateful for in the coming days.

A truckle bed was set up in Esther's room and her cousins took turns to sleep there in case she should call out in distress at night. During the day Charlotte and Harriet saw very little of each other, for the entry of one to the sick room was a signal for the other to depart.

That Harriet was seeing Mr Peacock every day was something which Charlotte was well aware of, and she could only be grateful that he was able to lift her spirits for a while. It was becoming increasingly obvious that Esther, far from improving, was extremely ill. The daily walks around the square with her swain at least gave Harriet some relief, and Charlotte stepped out for a short time each day with her abigail to bear her company.

The sisters would not leave Esther at the same time. Cosmo too called every day to enquire after the invalid, but it was Mr Harvey who haunted the house in St James's Square. Each day he brought a token and the house was filled with flowers but, unable to see Esther, the poor man was beside himself with worry. There was no doubt about how he felt. He told

Charlotte, "I should have declared myself ere long had this unfortunate situation not occurred. I desire nothing more in life than to be allowed to take care of Miss Meredith."

"I cannot answer for my cousin, of course," Charlotte replied, "but I am sure she will be only too happy to receive you when she is well again."

"And you take my messages to her?"

"Sadly she is in the grip of delirium and as such is not even aware of who I and my sister are. Naturally, as she improves I will convey your concern. The doctor comes each day to see her and I shall tell you immediately of any change, sir."

It was to a house in turmoil that Gresham paid a visit a day or so later. He was shocked to see how drawn Charlotte looked, and she came down from the sick room only for a few moments to receive him. "I cannot believe how much has occurred in the short time I have been away. Tell me, in how bad a case is your cousin?" he asked in his direct way.

"The doctor seems to be very grave when he visits. I can only take my lead from him. We are doing all we can, and we are praying."

"Then I shall add my prayers to your own and leave you in peace. Do please know that you must call on me if there is anything, anything at all that I can do. I shall return tomorrow to see how Miss Meredith goes on."

The visit, short as it was, brought some comfort to Charlotte. While Cosmo called every day, she did not feel in the light of recent events that she could burden him with her fears. Everyone else leaned on Charlotte, and the return of the Duke to London unaccountably made her feel better.

She returned to Esther's bedchamber, still afraid but lighter of foot as she climbed the stairs. The room felt strangely quiet.

She rushed to the bedside. The restlessness of her patient was gone and she lay as one ... no, Charlotte couldn't bear to think of it. She took Esther's lifeless hand and, sobbing, brought it to her lips.

Then she gasped. Could she be imagining it? But no, there was a slight pressure, barely discernible but definitely there. Her tears continued but this time they were of joy, for she realised the fever had broken. Hardly able to tear herself away, she knew she must send for the doctor. She pressed the bell and waited outside on the landing, the less to disturb Esther.

Giving instructions to the maid who answered her call, she went back into the room, seated herself beside her cousin, holding her hand all the while, and there she was to be found when the doctor arrived some half an hour later.

"You were quite right to call me, Lady Cranleigh, for the immediate danger is indeed past, but we must now put in place plans for Miss Meredith's return to full health. She will be very weak and even after the relief following the rain, London is still not the place for your cousin's convalescence. I would strongly advise you take her into the country, if that is possible. Perhaps to Bath where she may, as she regains her strength, take the water. She is not at present stout enough to travel, but in a week or so I am firmly of the opinion that she should be removed from the capital."

"Of course. I will set about making plans immediately. I cannot thank you enough, Doctor, for I am sure that without your aid Miss Meredith might well not have recovered."

The doctor smiled in acknowledgement of the compliment. "Continue, if you would, coaxing her to drink as much as possible. I see you have fresh lemonade on the side table there."

"My sister makes it for her."

"Then have her make as much as your patient will take, for it will only do her good. Introduce food gradually. She has not eaten for several days and will not want to face a meal. Find small things to tempt her appetite and I'm sure she will be better in no time at all. Do not at this stage encourage her to exert herself, for this is still a critical time and Miss Meredith's complete recovery will depend on how she goes along in the next week or so."

"Thank you, Doctor. My sister and I have the care of her and will ensure she is not allowed to take up the reins too quickly, as I know she would choose to do once she begins to feel better."

Charlotte escorted him to the front door. Before leaving he turned to her and said, "You have my card. I will come again if you call me, but I sincerely trust it will not be necessary. Goodbye, Lady Cranleigh."

"Goodbye, Doctor, and thank you."

She went back upstairs and turned her mind to the problem of getting Esther away from London. She was entirely unsure what to do for the best.

CHAPTER EIGHT

Not many minutes after the doctor had left, Harriet returned home with Mr Peacock.

"I will not detain you longer, as I am sure you wish to see how Miss Meredith has fared during your absence," he told her. "Be assured I will call again tomorrow."

"Thank you. I should have run mad, I think, had it not been for our daily walks. Charlotte still hardly leaves the house and I worry for her almost as much as for Esther."

"Your concern does you credit. I would wish I could … I think… No, now is not the time, Harriet," he said and, raising her hand to his lips, he left her somewhat abruptly, she staring after him from the doorstep.

Had he been going to declare himself? It seemed so, and even with all the troubles in the house Harriet's heart lifted. It was so like him to have held back. He was right, of course. It would have been entirely inappropriate for a declaration while Esther lay fighting for her life. It was the first time Harriet had acknowledged this, even to herself, and she raced upstairs with fear in her breast.

The room was bathed in sunlight, for Charlotte had drawn back the blinds and although the screen was still in place there was an entirely different air as Harriet entered. Her hand went to her throat in fear, but the smile on her sister's face was all she needed to know that the ordeal was now at an end. They moved together and embraced, and it was Harriet's turn to shed tears of relief.

Charlotte drew her to the window and spoke in hushed tones. "The doctor left but a few minutes ago. Esther is still very weak and he advises we remove her from London, not yet awhile but perhaps in a few days when she has regained a little strength. We must turn our minds to deciding where to go. He mentioned Bath."

Harriet looked bewildered and tried very hard to push away the selfish thoughts that presented themselves to her. Not for a moment would she have put her own wishes above the wellbeing of the woman who had stood as mother to her since she was a small child. If they must leave London, so be it. After their parting a few minutes earlier, she would retain faith in the depth of Quentin's feelings for her and hope they would not be separated for too long. She pushed away the despair and concentrated on trying to help her sister find a way out of their present difficulty.

Charlotte continued, "I cannot think Esther would like to return to Stapleton. Nor do I wish to ask my father. From things our cousin let slip from time to time, it seems she hadn't been happy there for many years and only remained out of loyalty to us."

"But where can we go, Charlotte? Would you choose Bath, perhaps, in the light of what the doctor said?"

"If we could find a suitable house to rent I'm sure it would serve the purpose, but I can't help thinking Esther would be more content in the country somewhere. Do you remember that she told us of how happy she was coming to Stapleton all those years ago when Mama was still alive? It is only latterly that she has fallen out of love with the place but not, I think, the rural life. She is a country woman at heart."

"Perhaps in a day or so, when she's feeling a little recovered, we might ask her preference."

Charlotte pondered on this for a moment but then put forward that it might burden her too much to think about it and it would be better to present her with a definite plan.

"I think you may be right. Ah well, we must set our minds to thinking of the best possible solution. In the meantime, you have not left the house for days. Now that we know Esther is out of danger, why don't you take Bess out for a ride? It will do you both good, for although I know your groom has been exercising her I am quite sure it isn't the same."

Feeling as if a huge burden had been lifted, Charlotte gave orders for Bess to be brought around in half an hour and went herself to change into her habit with eager anticipation.

As Charlotte cantered along the row, she came across Gresham walking in the park. He waved and she brought Bess to a halt beside him.

"What is this? I thought you didn't leave the house."

"Wonderful news, Your Grace. You will know that when you left me a while ago I was in a state of anxiety about my cousin. When I returned to her room, however, I found that the fever had broken. She has a long way to go but the doctor, whom I called immediately, of course, deems her to be out of danger. Harriet practically pushed me out of the house, insisting that I get some air and give Bess here an opportunity to stretch her legs."

"She certainly looked to be enjoying herself, as did you. May I help you down? Perhaps you might walk with me to the gate."

"I should be delighted, for I would ask your advice if I may."

As they walked, Charlotte explained her predicament. Gresham, it seemed, had the solution ready to hand, though there was some discussion before agreement was reached.

"Forgive me if I speak out of turn but, as well you know, Cranleigh stands empty. It would be an honour if you would consider spending the summer there with your sister and cousin. There is an abundance of things you could do. I believe I am right in thinking that you never went there with Ernest, but I can assure you there is much to please three ladies."

"I couldn't possibly agree to such a thing," she exclaimed.

"Why not?" he asked baldly.

"Because it isn't mine."

"No, it's mine and what a ridiculous situation it is. I have my own home. I cannot possibly occupy two mansions," he said, smiling, "and I can see no conceivable reason for your objection other than the one you have already put forward which, if you will forgive me saying so, is nonsensical."

"You take too much upon yourself," Charlotte responded more harshly than she meant to. The relief of knowing Esther was out of danger had given way to exhaustion and she spoke unguardedly.

"Not at all. Think of your patient. Would it not be in her best interests?"

She spluttered and was about to lose her temper when she realised the ridiculousness of the situation and instead burst into laughter.

"That's better, for I am sure you can see it makes sense."

"Indeed it does, and I cannot tell you how grateful I am, or how relieved. I believe it lies not far from Bath as well, so when Esther has improved somewhat it will still be possible to take her there."

"Good girl. I shall put the arrangements in place as soon as I can. Would it suit if I ask Quentin to accompany you? I am tied in London for a while, as my mother is here."

Charlotte came to a halt and Bess, whose bridle she was holding, was one pace ahead before she realised. Charlotte was pulled forward and would have stumbled had it not been for a steadying hand at her elbow. "Thank you. I had forgotten your mother was come to town. I must pay her a visit to express my thanks in person."

"You may do so tomorrow, if your sister will remain with Miss Meredith. I hope by then to have more to tell you."

"You are very kind."

"Nonsense!"

He sounded quite short with her. She wasn't sure she liked it. They had by this time reached the park gate, and Charlotte handed Bess into the care of her groom and allowed Gresham to escort her home.

"Until tomorrow, then," she said, offering her hand.

He took it and held it a fraction longer than was customary before responding "Tomorrow" and turning to leave.

Charlotte climbed the steps, reflecting that she did not find it offensive to have it thus, quite different from when Lord Roxburgh had performed the same action. It was hardly surprising that she felt some evil genius was at work when she entered the house to be told by her manservant that Lord Roxburgh himself awaited her in the morning room. It was with little enthusiasm that she went up to meet him.

"Good day, my Lord," she said, after taking a deep breath before entering the room. She was surprised to find him alone. Harriet, who had taken him in strong dislike, had chosen to remain with Esther rather than leave the sickroom for a guest.

"Good day, Lady Cranleigh. I hope you will forgive me waiting. Your sister was unable to join me, and I have only just heard of Miss Meredith's illness and am anxious to learn how she goes on."

"Please, do sit down." Charlotte indicated a chair and took one as far away as was politely possible. "Had you come yesterday you would have received very different tidings, but I am happy to say that my cousin is now out of danger and the priority is to ensure her speedy and full recovery."

"I am delighted to hear you say so. Does that mean I might have the pleasure of meeting you at the Stanfords' party this evening?"

"Good heavens, no indeed," she replied a little hastily. "We do not go out. In fact, we are hoping to leave town very soon, for the doctor thinks country air will be beneficial to our patient." She could have bitten her tongue but the words were out before she could stop them.

"Indeed. May I know where you mean to take her?"

"Our plans are not yet finalised. It has all happened in such a rush we find ourselves unprepared. We won't, however, be attending any social events before we leave. Neither I nor my sister will leave Miss Meredith in her present state." She rose and good manners dictated he did the same. "I hope we shall see you at the end of summer when we plan to return to town."

"With your permission, I shall make it my business to visit when you are settled in the country."

"As to that, I cannot say at the moment when we might be receiving callers, but it is kind of you to offer."

"You must know, Lady Cranleigh, that several weeks without seeing you will leave me dashed indeed. I do not try to hide my feelings, for you must know by now what they are, and I will not entreat you further at this time. I shall take my leave of you, but be assured you will be in my thoughts."

Lord Roxburgh left, but the chill that seemed to have enveloped Charlotte remained for some moments. Attempting to shrug it off she went in search of her sister, but she had little opportunity immediately to discuss the proposed plans with Harriet, for Roxburgh's departure was followed shortly by the arrival of Mr Peacock. When he too had left, she was able to tell her sister about Gresham's solution to their problem.

Harriet tried to mask the regret which involuntarily clouded her features. It turned to joy, however, on being informed that, if he would agree, Quentin would be acting as their escort into Wiltshire and thereafter she entered into the discussion with enthusiasm. "You will be able to practise your watercolours again, Charlotte. You know how much you enjoy them and how accomplished you are."

"Enjoy them, yes. Accomplished? No, for I fear I will never achieve Esther's skill. It may be perhaps that if the weather is clement she might take up her brushes into the park, which I believe to be very beautiful and quite extensive."

"And will Bess go with you?"

"Assuredly. It is my ambition to explore the grounds on her back."

"I envy you."

"Do not, for I have a small secret. The Duke of Gresham has brought back with him a gelding from his stables. If you approve, we will purchase him for you and he too will go with us."

Harriet was delighted. All she had to worry about now was that Quentin had no commitments that would prevent him acting as their escort.

CHAPTER NINE

When Charlotte visited the Duke's house in Berkeley Square the following morning accompanied by her maid, all was in a fair way to being arranged. They would leave a week hence if Esther should have improved sufficiently to travel. The Duke, as he informed her, had already sent word to Cranleigh to prepare to receive the party so Charlotte need not worry herself on that head.

"And now, may I take you to meet my mother? She has been asking me this past half hour if you are yet come."

Gresham led the way to a very nicely proportioned room on the next floor and stood back for Charlotte to enter. She went in with the assured air that came so naturally to her and approached the Duchess, who was seated on one side of a huge fireplace. "How kind of you to see me, Your Grace. You must know that I have been wanting for some time now to thank you in person for the gift of Bess. I know how difficult it must have been for you to part with her."

The Duchess offered both hands to her visitor and said, "Please forgive me if I do not stand. Sadly my body does not do as I would wish these days, and I am confined for much of the time to a chair. Not that I would wish people to regard me as an invalid." She was looking meaningfully at her son, who had joined them near the hearth. "I am well enough able to get about if I have time to prepare myself."

"Indeed you are, Mama. It's getting you to keep still in one place that proves most difficult."

"Surely the Duchess knows best what she can and cannot do," Charlotte remarked in her hostess's defence.

Gresham threw up his hands in defeat. "What chance do I have between the two of you? And yes, Mama, I will take you out in the barouche this afternoon if you wish."

"I do wish. I have been here for two days now and it's time I left the house. Perhaps you would care to join us, my dear?"

"If my sister stays with my cousin, I should be delighted. Would it please you for me to ride Bess and meet you in the park? You may then see her and my groom will take her home so I may join you in your carriage."

The suggestion was met not just with approval but with enthusiasm, and so it was arranged.

A few hours later, Charlotte reined in beside the carriage and greetings were exchanged. It was with difficulty that the older lady stepped out of the barouche with Gresham's help, but the temptation was too great for her not to caress her favourite, and if her eyes were a little bright nobody remarked on the fact. Bess pushed her muzzle into welcoming hands and the Duchess laid her cheek against that of the horse.

Charlotte was surprised to see such a look of care and deep devotion on Gresham's face, for she had been more used to seeing the spirited side of him. Certainly it did him no disservice in her eyes.

Some moments went by before the Duchess visibly pulled herself together and said with determination, "It seems we must part again, Bess. Be good to Lady Cranleigh, for I can see she is good to you and I have observed her light hands. There will be no tugging on the reins from that young lady. Join me in the carriage if you will, my dear, and Sebastian, do take Bess to her groom and give him this apple for her after her bridle has been removed."

Charlotte stood by the horse while Gresham helped his mother back into the carriage then, seeing the younger lady safely installed, he left them to talk, leading the mare away.

"You cannot know how nervous I have been, my dear. I have had Bess from a foal, you see, and though I trust my son's judgement implicitly in regard to horses, I could not quite be comfortable until I had seen you together. My mind is now at peace, and I can return to Gresham Hall with a lighter heart."

"I am nothing if not aware of the honour you do me, for Bess has the softest mouth and I can see how easy it would be to ruin that. As a child, any tendency I had to be heavy-handed was quickly beaten out of me, I can tell you."

"Beaten out of you?"

"No, not that of course, Your Grace, but I was soon made to realise that I would be harming my pony and that I could not bear."

"It has never ceased to surprise me how many riders will blame the horse for their own failings. It is something with which I have no patience."

"Nor I. Do you remain in London for long?"

"Not much above a week, I think, for my son needs to get back to the country."

"And are you desirous of returning so soon?"

"Yes, for while I enjoy seeing all my old friends, and they are kind enough to visit me in Berkeley Square, I cannot return the favour. To tell the truth, and I would not have you mention this to my son, I find each visit more of an ordeal than I like to admit. It may happen that this will be the last time I undertake such a journey."

"I am so sorry," said Charlotte, not knowing how else to respond.

"Oh, don't be. I am quite content at home. I would be delighted, though, if you could spend a few days with me there at some time. I would enjoy showing you some others of our horses. I don't have many visitors nowadays and certainly there are not many ladies who share my delight in them as I can see you do."

Charlotte was more flattered than she could say and had to confess to herself a certain curiosity to see this place of which she knew so little. "We go to Cranleigh next week, but if you are serious then I should be delighted to accept your kind offer after my cousin is sufficiently recovered from her illness to be left with my sister alone."

The ladies parted company, each more than pleased with the other, and a week later when the party from St James's Square removed to Cranleigh the Duchess and her son prepared to return to Gresham Hall.

The journey into Wiltshire took two days, for Esther could not have covered the distance in one. Vastly improved but still very weak, she was delighted with the accommodations the Duke, or rather his secretary, had arranged for them. Behind the superior inn they stopped at lay a very pretty garden. At the bottom ran a shallow stream which bubbled along over small boulders. It was close to this brook that Quentin had the landlord place some chairs and a small table. With the sun so high in the sky they were able to spend the remaining hours of daylight in happy companionship, even going so far as to partake of their dinner out of doors.

"What a delightful place this is," Harriet remarked. "I swear I could spend the rest of the summer here in such idyllic surroundings."

"It will not be so idyllic each time a coach pulls up for a change of horses or for its occupants to order some refreshment," Charlotte replied. "And for my part I cannot wait to see Cranleigh. Ernest told me little about it, and though there are paintings of it in the London house I am sure nothing will be quite the same as seeing it for myself."

"No indeed, and of course I am keen for the opportunity to ride Pageant properly for the first time. In fact, I think I might go now and see that he is comfortably stabled. You are aware that I have been visiting him daily during these past few days in London, and I am sure we are in a way to reaching a fine understanding. He is such a gentleman — and will do anything for a piece of apple."

"Yes, do go, and perhaps you could check on Bess for me at the same time? Mr Peacock, do accompany my sister if you please, for I do not like her to be alone while there are so many visitors to the inn with whom we are unacquainted."

It was kind of Charlotte to give the young couple some time together. The ladies had been cooped up in the carriage for much of the day, with Quentin riding alongside. There had been little opportunity for conversation.

They came back a while later to find Charlotte and her cousin returning from the garden to the inn. "Esther was beginning to flag a little and I deemed it time to get her to her bedchamber," Charlotte told them. "In fact, I too will retire, for we have another long day ahead of us tomorrow."

The party met again to partake of breakfast in the private parlour that had been set aside for them and they left soon after, excited and curious in varying degrees.

The weather in the country was much kinder and gentler than it had been in town and Esther's recovery moved on, if not speedily then certainly at a steady pace. Because none had been to Wiltshire before, it was an adventure for all. Ingram, the steward, undertook to escort one or all of them about the estate, depending upon what they wished to see and at what distance that might be found. The sisters rode together every morning and, freed from the restraints of riding in Hyde Park, Charlotte was able to go at a pace. Because Gresham had taken heed of what she'd said about Harriet's abilities as a rider, there was no question of her horse lagging behind. With each having a mount to whom they could do justice they tore around with abandon, careful only not to lead the horses into difficult ground and thereby risk their safety with an unexpected obstacle or ditch.

"Pageant is such a joy. I must remember to thank the Duke again for choosing such a splendid horse for me."

"We have both been lucky in that regard and owe him a great deal. His choice of mount for each of us has been faultless. That he has made Cranleigh available to us for the summer has removed such a weight from my mind that I cannot even put into words. It is an ideal place, is it not, for Esther to recuperate?"

"She grows better every day. I believe you were right when you said she prefers the country."

"I am sure of it. I believe it's why she first came to Stapleton all those years ago, for her parents spent much of their time in town and I don't think it suited her at all."

"Quentin seems to spend a lot of time with Ingram, does he not?" Harriet remarked as, on the third day of their visit, they were walking their horses back at a moderate pace after enjoying a great gallop.

"Apparently Gresham charged him with looking into a few things, for you must know he is not sure what will be best for the estate and he has no notion of selling it. Why, are you feeling neglected?"

"Of course not," Harriet protested, blushing slightly. "Only it seems that he has become very serious of late."

"But not when he is with you, my dear. His look, when it rests upon you, is as adoring as ever."

"Oh, do you really think so, Charlotte? I know you were wishful that I would meet many young men and perhaps I should not speak of it, but I could not look at another when my heart is already given."

"Don't look so tragic, my darling girl. There is no doubt that your affections are returned. I rather think Mr Quentin is waiting only for an opportunity to approach our father."

"Oh Charlotte, do you think so indeed?"

"Indeed I do."

The sisters were pleased, but perhaps not altogether surprised, to find a new guest had arrived at Cranleigh in their absence. Mr Harvey was lodging at an inn nearby and came to see how the ladies did. He hoped he was not inconveniencing them. "Miss Meredith is looking well, don't you think? The country air is beneficial to her?"

"It is, and I am certain your visit can only be good for her," Charlotte replied. "I was sorry to have to turn you away when we were in London, but we felt complete quiet was necessary at that time. There is no doubt, though, that when you were able to call during the week prior to our departure it cheered her immensely."

"I had hoped it would be so."

Charlotte glanced over to where Esther was sitting, apparently deep in conversation with Harriet and Quentin, but her cousin was under no illusion. Esther was very aware of the presence of the newcomer and the colour in her cheek was evidence of such.

"Do you have business in the area, Mr Harvey?" Charlotte continued.

"Not at all. London was becoming unbearable and, as I knew your direction, I took the liberty of coming into Wiltshire to see how you were all getting along."

"Do you plan to stay long?"

George Harvey looked a trifle abashed before disclosing that he did not know the duration of his visit. "I thought no further than to come here," he confessed.

"Then why do you not remove from the inn and join our party? The Duke bade me invite any friends I liked and it will be tedious for you to be going back and forth."

Harriet, who had heard this part of the conversation, cried out, "What a splendid idea! Do join us, sir!"

The rest added their entreaties and it was arranged. Mr Harvey, who had ridden over on a hired hack, would return to the inn as he had planned, but Quentin would drive over the following day to collect him and his baggage.

The next few days were given over solely to pleasure as the gardens near the house were explored and, as Esther regained her strength, they ventured further into the park and the home wood. No heavy showers occurred to spoil their enjoyment. With her companions forming naturally into two couples,

Charlotte sometimes felt a little *de trop*, but she would not for a single moment have conveyed her discomfiture to the rest.

One morning after her ride, Charlotte, not wishing to go with the rest who had determined to find out if the trout were as bountiful as promised, ventured into parts of the house she had not yet seen. She found herself in a long galleried room with intricate plasterwork to the ceiling, which was hung with several chandeliers at regular intervals. The whole of one wall was given over to windows, the spaces in between filled with, she considered, rather ugly ornate pieces of furniture, one of which supported the most hideous vase she had ever seen.

She turned to the facing wall, which was covered with paintings of the Cranleigh dynasty in every guise. Some were portraits, others family groups. She sought and soon found one of Ernest. He sat astride a magnificent-looking hunter, and she knew he must have been pleased with this representation. He had been, she had to admit, a quite handsome man and the artist had captured all that was the best of him.

"How sad that you should have died so young," Charlotte exclaimed aloud, then looked about guiltily, for her voice had echoed in that huge chamber. There was none to hear her, though, and she moved on, examining the name of each subject as she went, trying to acquaint herself with the ancestors of her late husband. She was startled when she chanced upon a small portrait of the Duke of Gresham, painted, she judged, some ten years earlier. There was a softness about him that the years between had eradicated, the innocence of youth depicted well.

The door opened to admit Ingram who, having come in search of her, said, "I was wondering, Ma'am, if you would like me to give you any guidance. It can be confusing, I know, with such a large family."

"That is kind of you, Mr Ingram, but I was about to come down, for I have just observed through the window that the others are returning."

He stood back to allow her to pass in front of him. "I hope you have enjoyed what you've seen, for I am mindful that, forgive me if I speak out of turn, had circumstances been otherwise, this would have been your home."

"Thank you, that is very thoughtful of you."

"I would have been, indeed I am, proud to serve you, Lady Cranleigh."

Charlotte was a little overcome, having no idea of the degree of loyalty her self-possession and dignity had already inspired in this most senior of her late husband's staff. Her thoughts were jumbled as she descended the grand stairway. Had Ernest lived, all this would have been hers. Instead, it had passed to his cousin who maintained, if he were to be believed, that he didn't desire it at all. And she did believe him. She might not always like his manners, he could be short to the point of rudeness sometimes, but that he always told the truth she was sure. She'd been surprised for a moment when she'd come upon his portrait, forgetting there was such a close family connection. Thinking of him now, and moving across the hall to meet the rest, she found she was missing his company. *And why should I not?* she thought. *He is a man of good sense, after all.*

She pushed aside thoughts of Gresham and smiled in welcome. "I smell fish. Distinctly I smell fish. Well, was it all you hoped it would be?" she asked Harriet.

"Even better. Mr Harvey has a great talent and showed us all the way. You shall sample our catch, for we are determined to have them for our supper."

"Thank you, Harriet. Meanwhile I beg you will all go and wash your hands, for I can assure you I do not wish you to come into the drawing room like that," she teased them.

"And tomorrow Mr Harvey and Mr Peacock are to shoot rabbits and we are to take our easels into the shrubbery and paint, are we not, Esther?"

Esther, who was fast recovering her strength and spirits, smiled at her young cousin's enthusiasm. She was, however, concerned for Charlotte, detecting that she was unsettled, beneath her gaiety.

A little over a week into their stay at Cranleigh, the party were sitting in the shade of a huge oak enjoying the various delicacies that had been set before them, picnic style, should they happen to feel the pangs of hunger before their next meal. There was barely a ripple on the lake, which was visible from their vantage point, but the temperature was quite comfortable, provided they remained beneath the canopy of the tree. Charlotte raised her hand to shield her eyes as, looking in the direction of the house, she could see figures approaching. Her ready smile turned to stone as she recognised the man who was being escorted by one of the footmen. She rose to greet him, schooling her features, but her breath was tight in her breast.

"Viscount Roxburgh, how kind of you to call. I wasn't aware that you had our direction."

"My dear Lady Cranleigh, you must know that I was concerned for Miss Meredith. Good afternoon, Miss Meredith. I am delighted to see you making such progress. Miss Willoughby. Your servant, Peacock and erm…" he said, turning to the man who was to him a stranger.

Charlotte introduced George Harvey and had willy-nilly to invite Lord Roxburgh to join them.

"I was fortunate to bump into Fortescue a few days ago, and he it was who informed me of your whereabouts. Naturally, I came as soon as circumstances permitted to see if there was any way I could be of service to you."

"How thoughtful of you. We have been keeping to the house and grounds. It is too soon for my cousin to be venturing very far."

Roxburgh included himself in the general conversation as if he had been part of the group and was oblivious to the fact that each member wished him elsewhere. After a while, he begged Lady Cranleigh to take a turn with him. "For the grounds here are, I can see, quite beautiful."

Charlotte reluctantly consented, and they walked towards a small copse situated a short distance away. Once within the shelter of the trees, Roxburgh abandoned all pretence and clasped Charlotte's hands.

"My dearest Lady Cranleigh, you cannot but be aware how I feel, for I have already told you as much. Now that your cousin is on the mend, I have made it my business to come and see you in the hope that you will look kindly upon my suit." He astonished her further by dropping to one knee and asking her to marry him. "I have loved you almost from the moment I first saw you."

Charlotte felt only revulsion and, when he sprang up and clasped her in his arms, she managed to break free and exclaim, "My lord, you forget yourself." Her breathing came fast and she was more than a little frightened. Looking around, she was about to call for help when he stepped back.

"Forgive me. My feelings overcame me. I did not mean to cause your distress. Forgive me," he said again.

"I am sorry, but I cannot return your affections. Please, I beg you, do not speak of this again."

"But think, my dearest," he continued, not finished yet, "it is obvious that your sister will marry Mr Peacock, and Mr Harvey seems more than fond of Miss Meredith. It may be that you will find yourself alone, and I would give you the protection of my name."

"You are presumptuous, sir. I need no such protection. I must ask you to leave. There can be no further reason for you to remain, and I must return to my sister and my cousin."

Roxburgh bowed stiffly and walked towards the house, departing without a word to the rest.

All Charlotte's pleasure in the day was gone, and it took the combined efforts of her companions to coax her out of her restlessness.

"What say we play lawn bowls?" Harriet asked. "You know how much we used to enjoy it at Stapleton."

"It's far too hot to be standing in the full sun."

"You are right, Charlotte, but we could return inside and have a game of spillikins," Esther suggested.

There was no distracting her and the two gentlemen looked a little uncomfortable, for Lady Cranleigh was obviously much distressed. That they could only put down to her encounter with Lord Roxburgh, last seen striding off in a temper.

"Please excuse me. I am not in good frame at present. Permit me to compose myself and I will join you again later."

Mr Peacock, who already held his lordship in strong dislike, was all for chasing after him, but Charlotte would allow no such confrontation. Mr Harvey too was concerned that Roxburgh might return and broke in hesitantly, "Perhaps, if I may suggest… Miss Meredith is much improved. I wonder if we might remove to Bath for a few days so she may take the waters. It is close by. I would undertake to ride there and enquire if we can find rooms at one of the hotels. I believe there are several fine establishments."

Charlotte doubted Roxburgh would show his face again, but it was as if Mr Harvey had had recourse to a lucky charm. Not just Charlotte but the whole group were animated by his proposition. All eyes turned anxiously upon Esther, for she it was who must have the final say in this matter. She looked at Mr Harvey with gratitude, exclaiming, "What a wonderful idea. I didn't like to say it, but I must admit to a sense of the fidgets. It is unlike me to be inactive for so long. Beautiful as it is here, I believe it would be beneficial to us all to visit Bath. I have never been, and I know neither Charlotte nor Harriet have taken the water nor visited the Pump Room."

"No, nor anything else, Esther. Thank you, Mr Harvey, for you have found the cure for my ill-humour."

And so it was arranged. Within two days, George Harvey had bespoken rooms for them all and returned to Cranleigh to escort the ladies to that famous watering hole.

CHAPTER TEN

Mr Harvey had been fortunate indeed in procuring lodgings in Henrietta Street, for at this time of year Bath, though not as popular as it had been in the past, was brim-full of people, both residents and visitors. The ladies were delighted with the situation, convenient as it was for so many of the city's attractions and but a short walk to Sydney Gardens. It had been agreed they would remain for some two weeks, for there was much to see.

"And if we cross Pulteney Bridge it is barely a few steps to Milsom Street, where I have been informed the shops are excellent," Harriet enthused.

"That also is my understanding, Harriet," Charlotte replied, "but if we take a different direction, we shall find ourselves close to the Abbey and the Pump Room. Perhaps we ought first to pay them a visit. Esther, what do you think? Are you agreeable to taking the water?"

"As I understand its benefits are highly thought of, I am inclined to think I must try, though I believe the taste to be quite unusual."

There was much discussion about the things they should do, amongst the ladies and gentlemen both. All were united in their determination to attend the Assembly Rooms, for there were ample pursuits to entertain them there.

"I believe it holds upwards of one thousand people," Harriet said with round-eyed astonishment. "There is dancing, and tea, and I have been told they hold concerts there as well," she added.

"You had that last from me," said Mr Peacock, "though I have never been myself, so it may just be hearsay. But I am assured there is a card room."

It was evident that all concerned were looking forward to some days of unalloyed pleasure. Charlotte's spirits had lifted since they'd arrived and she was anxious to put behind her the incident that had so upset her and to take advantage of everything Bath had to offer. Esther smiled to see her entering into plans with enthusiasm. She was female enough to wish to see what was on hand in the superior shops the city was famous for.

Their visit to the Pump Room had proved to be one of mixed blessings, Esther having, after one sip, declared the water undrinkable, though she made a remarkable show of pretending to do so. She was grateful when George Harvey, noticing her predicament, removed the glass from her hands and discreetly disposed of it.

"That was kind of you. I was at a loss to know what to do with it."

"Any service I can do for you, small though it may be, can only give me pleasure."

"Charlotte? Is that you, Charlotte?"

Charlotte turned in delight to greet Maria Stanford. "Maria! How lovely. I had no notion you were here in Bath."

"Nor I you. I understood you were fixed for some time at Cranleigh."

"Indeed we were, but how could we be so near and not undertake such an easy journey while we were in the vicinity? You know everyone, don't you? Oh no, allow me to introduce Mr George Harvey, a friend of ours to whom we are indebted for securing accommodation for us during our stay."

Lady Stanford seated herself beside Esther and engaged her and Mr Harvey in conversation for a short while before dragging Charlotte off to meet some old acquaintances. They walked the length and back again of the beautifully proportioned room with its high ceilings and grand columns, softened at each end by a curved alcove. It took some time, for they paused here and there to engage in conversation with some of the other visitors. Here it was where people went to see and be seen, and Charlotte felt it fulfilled its expectation admirably.

The next day Esther declared that, glad though she was to have been, it wouldn't grieve her if she didn't return to the Pump Room. "There is so much else to do, so, though I am grateful for the experience, I do not feel it needs to be repeated."

"Yes, it was nice to see Maria, for I am immensely fond of her but to be walking up and down in such a crush is not entirely to my taste, though I believe there are those who go every day," Charlotte said. "I myself prefer smaller, more intimate gatherings." Now where had she heard that before?

"It most certainly won't be a small and intimate gathering at the Assembly Rooms," Harriet said. "Do you not wish to go after all?"

Charlotte looked at her sister, whose face bore a regretful expression but which lit up again when Charlotte assured her that she wouldn't miss it for the world. "Isn't it lucky we packed suitable attire, for on so short a visit we might not have anticipated such an opportunity? However, I feel certain we should regret it if we didn't make it our business to go there."

It was agreed by all that the evening spent at the Assembly Rooms was by far the most enjoyable of their whole stay in Bath. Though prepared for the magnificence of the ballroom, the sheer size took each of them by surprise. By comparison, the Pump Room was positively dwarfed. They began by joining the dancers, and even in the crowd Charlotte could see many of her London acquaintance. She was delighted, though, when she recognised Cosmo Fortescue making his way towards her.

"I had no idea you were in Bath, Cosmo. What a happy chance to have met you here."

"I have come only on a short visit and had been hoping to call on you at Cranleigh to apologise before journeying into Berkshire to see my family."

"Apologise?"

"I fear you may have received a visit from Lord Roxburgh. I'm afraid that I was careless enough to give him your direction."

"Yes, he told me so. There is no need of an apology, though, for without his visit we might not have come to Bath. I would then neither have experienced its pleasures nor met you here."

Mr Fortescue was more than a little relieved. Knowing as he did of her aversion to Roxburgh, he had been concerned that she may have been much distressed.

"I should be delighted to see you while we are in Wiltshire," Charlotte continued. "We return to Cranleigh in a day or two, and it would give me such pleasure if you could join us."

Charlotte had fallen into her natural way of talking to Cosmo and was glad he hadn't distanced himself from her. It had come home to her of late that she now had a wide social circle but few intimate friends. Her imagination still failed her when she tried to plan her future. Not one to repine, she had tried to push these thoughts into the background and the visit to Bath had certainly succeeded in lifting her spirits.

"Sadly I have received news today that my father is quite unwell, and I cannot further delay my journey. I must leave tomorrow. I make no excuse, therefore, for monopolising you for the rest of the evening," he said, smiling. "Would you care to play cards before tea?"

"Oh yes, above all things. It is such a long time since I've played. I fear you will find me a little rusty."

He bore her off to the card room where they spent a happy hour playing piquet, leaving Harriet dancing with Quentin and Esther with Mr Harvey.

Upon leaving the hall, Charlotte had noticed as she passed her cousin that she was looking a little drawn and wondered if perhaps Esther was doing too much too quickly.

Esther's pallor, though, had nothing to do with her recent sickness. George, unable to contain himself any longer, had offered her his heart and his hand. They had been sitting aside from the rest, unobserved, when the words it seemed were forced from him.

"Esther, I beg you will do me the honour of becoming my wife. I had not dreamed that at my age love would come to me. I cannot feel that you are indifferent to me, for we have come to know each other well these past few weeks. I wouldn't have spoken yet, but it seems that you are quite recovered now." He hesitated, for there had been no response from the lady other than a slight tightening of her hand within his. "I have spoken too soon. Forgive me."

"No, George, not that. Only I fear you will not understand. I have been so happy in your company that I have disregarded what was happening around me, within my own family. One cannot doubt that Harriet and Mr Peacock will make a match of it, and soon. She and Charlotte have been in my care for so long now and I can only delight in her joy. But I cannot leave Charlotte alone. She has been through so much. George, it would be the greatest honour for me to become your wife but, and I pray you will comprehend, I must decline."

"But surely Lady Cranleigh will remarry in time?"

"It may be that she will, though she declares she does not wish to. Until she does, I can only beg that you perceive my dilemma." Esther's eyes filled with unaccustomed tears, but by force of will she held them from falling.

"I understand that you feel a mother's love and I am past the age of youthful impatience. Do not upset yourself, dearest. If you will permit, we will continue as before and hope that in time we will be able to be together as I would wish. For now, let us put this aside and join the rest of the dancers. It will cheer us both."

So it was that when Charlotte had left the room with Mr Fortescue she quite misread the reason Esther was looking so wan. By the time they all met up again for tea, her cousin was much recovered and able to enjoy the rest of the evening.

"I am so sadly out of practice that Mr Fortescue, in what I can only regard as a very unchivalrous manner, beat me at every game," Charlotte said, attempting to look woebegone but with a twinkle in her eyes.

"And I have no doubt, my dear lady, that you would have fleeced me unmercifully had the cards not fallen my way. I would give much for another opportunity to try our skills against each other."

"Oh yes," Harriet said excitedly. "Why can we not play, all of us, when we return to Cranleigh? I cannot imagine why we have not done so before."

"Regretfully, Mr Fortescue is unable to accompany us. However, when we are once again settled in London I shall have no hesitation in organising a card party in the hope I may have my revenge."

"A challenge I shall accept with alacrity. In the meantime, may I thank you all for a very entertaining evening. I shall look forward to seeing you again in St James's Square."

CHAPTER ELEVEN

The ladies paid one more visit to Milsom Street before leaving Bath. "There was the most delightful ribbon in my favourite shade of green, and I regretted almost immediately that I didn't purchase it when we were there," Charlotte had said.

"And that parasol which I so admired but felt to be such an extravagance. I have been thinking it would be the very thing when walking in the grounds at Cranleigh when the sun is so bright," Harriet responded.

Esther found a trimming for one of her bonnets which cheered her immensely and the three ladies returned to their lodging very well satisfied with their morning's work. The day was still young and fine so it was decided that, accompanied by Mr Peacock and Mr Harvey, they should take advantage of the weather to enjoy a walk in Sydney Gardens. Harriet felt this would be the perfect opportunity to try out her new parasol and straight away removed it from its wrappings. Charlotte would have it that they must enter The Labyrinth, a treat which was declined by Esther and the two gentlemen but seized upon by Harriet. The young women spent a happy time seeking to resolve the maze, trying first this path and then that until much against Charlotte's inclination they asked for directions to the exit and re-joined their companions.

The sisters, escorted by Mr Quentin, had been to admire the architecture of The Circus and Royal Crescent but Esther had declined, saying she was quite fagged to death and wasn't sure that she could manage the steep climb. The truth was that she couldn't hide innermost feelings from her cousins for long stretches at a time, and she was determined they should not learn of her sacrifice.

"I shall save my energy for tomorrow, when we are to go to the Abbey."

"You missed such a treat, Esther," Charlotte told her upon their return. "I wished I'd had my sketchbook with me. The beauty and lines of the buildings were something to behold and the view from Royal Crescent across the valley of the River Avon was quite spectacular."

She and Harriet had been touched by Mr Peacock's concern when he had desired to hire a chair to carry them up the hill. He hadn't considered that for two young women raised in the country walking wasn't merely a gentle social activity but something to be embraced with enthusiasm.

On the following morning all five made the short walk to the Abbey. Esther, having regained her health and her composure, gave no sign of the heartache she was feeling, and with Mr Harvey was still in attendance her cousins had no reason to think anything was amiss. They had all had the opportunity of admiring the exterior of Bath Abbey when visiting the Pump Room which was in such close proximity. Once inside they separated, each choosing to explore on their own. They found much to marvel at in the design and structure of a building which had undergone considerable change in its hundreds of years. The stained glass windows were at once breath-taking and awe-inspiring. Above all there was a hush about the place that induced a feeling of peace, and each paused for some moments in private prayer.

Harriet, who had been much moved, remarked as they left, "Of all things it is what I should desire to see again if I return to Bath."

"Would that be before or after you visit the shops in Milsom Street?" Charlotte teased, lightening a mood which had become almost sombre.

The next day they left Bath, and though the journey into Wiltshire was a little tedious they whiled away the time talking of all the things they had recently experienced. It came as a surprise to them all on arriving at Cranleigh to find the Duke of Gresham had taken up residence in their absence. Charlotte was surprised to find how pleased she was to see him, asserting to herself that a party of six would be more balanced and she could cease feeling *de trop*. The truth was that she had missed their conversations, lively sometimes for the wrong reasons but always entertaining.

"Good to see you, Gresham," Quentin said, shaking his friend warmly by the hand. "Have you been here long?"

"Above a week now. Ingram informed me you had all gone to Bath and, though I was tempted to follow you, I had much to do. He is an exceptional steward and I have learned a lot from him these past few days. And did you enjoy your visit, Lady Cranleigh?"

"Yes, and spent far too much on fripperies I might well have done without. The shops on Milsom Street are all they are said to be. I loved the elegance of the Pump Room, though my cousin found the water not to her taste. We all enjoyed our visit to Sydney Gardens, and the Abbey and, oh, any number of things. And to think, if it hadn't been for Viscount Roxburgh putting me in a bad skin, we might never have gone."

"Roxburgh was here?" Gresham exclaimed, a frown marring his features. Charlotte, even knowing there was no love lost between the two men, was surprised at the revulsion in his voice. "That was an unwarrantable intrusion. How came he to know your direction?"

Charlotte chose not to point out that Gresham had himself told her she might welcome anyone she liked to Cranleigh, not the least because Roxburgh had not in fact been welcome. "Naturally we did not invite him. It seems he encountered Mr Fortescue in London. It was he who gave Viscount Roxburgh our direction, though he has told me since he could have wished the words unsaid."

"You've seen Cosmo as well?"

"Yes, he spent a day or two in Bath before visiting his family in the country. Berkshire, I think he said."

Gresham turned to Esther, remarking that she was looking in much better health since last he had seen her.

"Thank you, and so I should, for they have all been wrapping me in wool. Mr Harvey here in particular … you are acquainted?"

"Yes, we met in St James's Square before you left town."

"Well, it was Mr Harvey who had the happy idea of removing us all to Bath. Lady Cranleigh was discomposed by the Viscount's visit and the suggestion was put forward in a bid to raise her spirits. I make no bones in telling you, for you already know, that gentleman is not a favourite with any of us."

The group dispersed to change for dinner. No more mention was made of Roxburgh until the following day when Charlotte found herself alone with Quentin in the breakfast room, the others not having yet put in an appearance.

"This antipathy between Gresham and Roxburgh is of long standing, I believe?" Charlotte spoke the words not as a statement but as a question.

"Yes, it is something he chooses not to talk about, but there is a hatred there that stays with him still."

"Hatred? A strong word."

"But in this case, I think, justified. It was some ten years ago. Try to imagine if you would a group of young men full of spirit and ready for any lark. Sebastian and his cousin Bertram — his cousin on his mother's side, no relation to Ernest — were two such bucks. Cockfighting, hunting, racing, boxing. All were pursuits which they entered into with the enthusiasm any fresh from university will do."

"How does this involve Roxburgh?"

"He was two years their senior and an habitual gamester. A successful one too. Though none has ever accused him of cheating, it certainly appeared that the luck was out of common on his side."

Charlotte glanced at the door, hoping none would enter before Mr Peacock had finished his tale.

"Bertram was caught up in his coils. He'd been dipping deep for some time, but one evening — Gresham was visiting his mother at Gresham Hall at the time — the stakes were driven higher and higher. Roxburgh's doing by all accounts, and Bertram full of bravado and following where he led. By the end of the night he was a broken man. He had signed away everything. Others who were there tried to put a stop to it but Roxburgh just laughed them off, saying that if the lad was old enough to play he was old enough to pay."

"And Gresham carries his hate to this day because of his cousin's ruin?"

"Oh no. He would of course have been disdainful of a man with a few more years under his belt who ought perhaps to have known better. Gresham might not then have admired him, but he wouldn't have loathed him as he does. No, it was what happened next that put the seal on it."

Anxious now to hear the rest, Charlotte unconsciously leaned forward in her seat. "What did happen next?"

"Like I said, Bertram was a broken man. He had lost his home, his pride and, above all, his self-respect. He went home and put a bullet through his head."

"Oh no!"

"Gresham returned to town the next day in time only to arrange the funeral. He sought out everyone who had been present on that fateful evening and each gave the same version of events. Gresham was more hot-headed in those days, but even he knew that he had no grounds upon which to challenge Roxburgh. It seemed to all observers that the play was above board. There is no doubt, however, that Gresham holds Roxburgh responsible for his cousin's death."

"No wonder," Charlotte remarked, remembering something Gresham had once said to her. At the time it had seemed the words were forced from him. Now she knew why he had spoken them. *Don't play with Roxburgh.*

"So you see, my dearest one, I must go to London to speak to your father," Quentin said earnestly, holding both Harriet's hands tightly in his own. "Now that Gresham is here to act as host, I must reluctantly leave you."

Harriet returned his grasp, tears on the ends of her lashes as she reflected upon all he had told her. He could wait no longer to declare himself to the world. No more was he prepared to watch other men paying court to her. He wanted their betrothal to be announced as soon as could be.

"Gresham has offered me the management of his estate here at Cranleigh," Quentin told her. "He is too occupied at Gresham Hall to take care of it himself, and he does not want to sell it, so he offered me a tenancy for life in exchange for me running things here."

They would live at Cranleigh if it pleased her. If it didn't, he would buy her a home in whichever part of the country she chose to reside. Everything had come so quickly and it all seemed a bit unreal, standing as they were in the rose garden with the scent of those beautiful flowers filling the air.

"I never thought to live here, but it's what I should like above all things. I have in these few weeks grown to love the place and I can perfectly well see why the Duke would wish to leave it in a safe pair of hands." Her grip tightened even more. "My only concern is that Charlotte might not like it."

"Yes, I understand. She could hardly live with us in a house that in other circumstances would have been hers."

Harriet smiled that he might think her sister would stay with them after her marriage. "She would never consider living with us here or indeed in any other house, Quentin."

"But it's what you did when she married Cranleigh," he said, not understanding why it should be different when the boot was on the other leg, so to speak.

"That was more in the nature of a rescue. She knew I could not live any longer with my father at Stapleton."

Harriet had long ago explained to Quentin how distant her father had been all their lives, how insupportable life would have been without her sister and cousin. She had been so lonely stuck in the country without them, even for that short time.

"You would be stuck in the country here."

"But I should not be lonely," she said, smiling. "In any case, you have a house in town which I am sure we would visit from time to time. Then Bath, of course, is close to hand with all it has to offer. For the most part, though, I prefer the country and would like, if it is permitted, to help you with your work. I have some experience, having been about the estate with Charlotte when she was managing Stapleton."

"Then I shall speak to Gresham before I leave. Tell him we shall come to Cranleigh just as soon as can be. Shall we tell your sister?"

"I think we should tell her that you go to London to see my father. I believe it will come as no shock to her. For the rest, I think it best if I confide in her when we are alone, for it will be as much of a surprise to her as it was to me."

"Then let us go in and join the others, for I cannot wait to tell them all that you have consented to be my wife."

There had been much rejoicing though no exclamations of surprise when the couple returned to the house.

Later that evening Charlotte and Esther joined Harriet in her bedchamber as they were about to retire.

"I am so happy for you, Harriet. I once said, you may remember, that I would have you marry for love. There can be no doubt that you and Quentin are so captivated with each other that the rest of the world may go where it will. I remember when first we met him at Maria Stanford's soiree. Though he was very polite to me and to Esther too, he could not tear his eyes from you."

"Indeed I feel I might live happily with him on a desert island."

"Until you require some ribbon for your bonnet or a new reticule," Esther put in, smiling fondly at her young cousin. "A desert island would be less than convenient then, I think. But what of this proposal that you live at Cranleigh?"

Harriet had told her sister and cousin of Gresham's plans to give Quentin the tenancy at Cranleigh, while looking apprehensively at Charlotte to see if she might have reservations about this employment of her late husband's estate. She need not have worried.

"Ernest would, I am sure, have been delighted to know that his home will be put to good use. Though I never came here with him, he had been planning a visit shortly before he passed away. He spoke of Cranleigh with such pleasure and took great pride in the fact that his family had worked the land for generations."

"And you don't object to my being here in your place?" Harriet asked anxiously.

Charlotte was surprised by the question. It had never been her home and, while she could appreciate its magnificence, she had no sentimental feelings about the house and its surroundings. "My place was never here, Harriet. Do not think it. I am happy only that you will have the life you deserve. And maybe," she added with an impish smile, "I might be able to stay in the Dower House when I become old and infirm."

The party sorely felt the loss of one of its members for, although Gresham was there in Quentin's stead, he was busy about the estate for much of the time. Esther was by this time completely recovered and it was decided, having been several weeks away, that they would all, Gresham excepted, return to London. Harriet was naturally anxious to know the outcome of Quentin's interview with her father, and George Harvey admitted there were several things he needed to attend to, some of which were becoming pressing.

"Thank you, Your Grace, for your kindness in letting us remain here all this time," Charlotte said. "With my cousin fully restored to health, I am sure you will be glad to see the back of us."

"Not at all, Lady Cranleigh. You are welcome at any time, here or at Gresham Hall. In fact, I am hoping you will give my mother the pleasure of your company before long."

"I should like that of all things. Once my sister's future is settled, I would be delighted to accept your kind offer."

"Then I shall see to it that arrangements are made. Goodbye, then. For now."

Gresham raised her hand to his lips then took her arm as he escorted her to the waiting carriage. Charlotte turned to smile up at him before entering the carriage.

"Thank you once again, for I do not know what we would have done these past weeks without your hospitality." She realised with regret that she would miss him and, with an inward sigh, she joined her companions.

CHAPTER TWELVE

Quentin had sought and found Sir Archibald Willoughby at Fenton's Hotel, but the man was in a sorry state. He was dishevelled and quite obviously a trifle disguised and, had he been able to do so, Mr Peacock would have excused himself and come back at another time. Harriet's father was, however, quite determined that his visitor join him.

"Come in, dear boy. I could do with some company. I do so hate to drink alone."

"I could return another day, sir, if it would be more convenient."

"Not at all. I insist. Erm, do I know you?"

There was nothing for it but to chance his arm. Accepting the drink that was offered, he introduced himself. "My name is Quentin Peacock. I am acquainted with your daughter."

"Charlotte?"

"No, your younger daughter, Harriet. We have formed an attachment over the past several weeks, and it is my earnest wish that she become my wife. I am here to ask that you look kindly upon my suit, for I have loved her from the moment we met and I promise you I will take every care of her." The words came out in a somewhat stilted manner, his sangfroid, in his anxiety, having completely deserted him.

The older man looked up sharply, torn it seemed from something else that appeared to be distracting him. "Well, well, well. Little Harriet, eh? I hope you're a rich man. Peacock, did you say? For I cannot provide her with a dowry. I'm in the suds to be sure. You are lucky to find me here at all, in fact. I have been playing rather deeply and must repair to the country to retrench. I am returning to Stapleton first thing tomorrow to put my affairs in order."

Quentin was not at all sure he wanted to be made the recipient of this much information but there was no stopping the man.

"It was the cards, you see," Sir Archibald ploughed on. "Thought I could bring myself about. Been lucky before. No reason why I shouldn't have been again."

The man's speech was slurred, and Quentin tried not to show his distaste. He'd been in his cups himself from time to time, after all, though only once or twice in his salad days. It was evident from Sir Archibald's complexion — red nose, broken blood vessels — that he was no stranger to strong liquor, and in large quantities at that. Quentin had a stab at sympathy. "I'm sorry to hear that, sir. Perhaps if you hold rein for a bit…"

But Sir Archibald interrupted him mid-sentence and jumped up, staggering as he did so and knocking over his chair. "The man's a devil. Kept urging me on. 'Just another hand,' he kept saying. And by the end of the night, I'd lost everything I own. My vowels are in Roxburgh's hands, and he's not the sort to be prepared to wait long for me to redeem them. In any case, how could I?"

"Roxburgh, you say?"

This was information Quentin would have preferred not to know. He thought it to be of too private a nature to be shared on such short acquaintance, and his prior knowledge of Roxburgh led him to agree with Sir Archibald's assessment. However, judging by the state of the man, it was possible he would not even remember the conversation in the morning. In the meantime, Quentin righted the chair, urged Sir Archibald once more to be seated and pressed ahead. "Then I am happy to have found you here before your imminent departure. I am sorry for your predicament, but I would like to reassure you that I am able to provide for your daughter in a manner that you would wish, sir." Quentin then acquainted Sir Archibald with such of his circumstances as he considered he needed to know.

There was a pause while Sir Archibald seemed to be trying to digest this information. "Little Harriet," he said again. "Well, I wish you joy, my boy, and here's my hand on it." It seemed the matter was arranged, the older man's mind obviously being on other things.

"Would you like me to carry any message back to her?" Quentin asked.

Sir Archibald made an effort to pull himself together. "Send her a father's love and tell her I wish her happy. Come, let's drink a toast." He poured with a shaking hand, more of the blood-red liquid spilling onto the table than going into the glasses.

Quentin left as soon as he was politely able to do so and hoped he would have to see little of his father-in-law in the future. He did not like the man and could perfectly understand why his daughters held him in little affection. But Roxburgh? It was none of his business, of course, but his worry was how this knowledge might impact on Harriet and Charlotte.

Quentin did not speak of her father's situation with Harriet. He was loath to burden her with the knowledge of something she could do so little about. His betrothed having approved of the wording in the announcement of their engagement, it was sent to the *Morning Post* and thereafter it seemed they had little time to themselves, what with friends calling to offer their felicitations and invitations to them to join various parties or entertainments. Harriet was as excited as any young bride ought to be as they made plans for their wedding, to take place within a few weeks, for why would they wait?

"We have today been to look at houses, as Quentin is of the opinion that his present residence is not suitable for a married couple," she said excitedly to Charlotte in the short time they had to converse between her return from that expedition and repairing to her chamber for a change of raiment prior to the evening's activities. "How much more pleasant London is now the hot weather has abated," she remarked, failing to attribute her pleasure to circumstances rather than climate.

Charlotte delighted in seeing her sister so happy. "It will be quiet after Harriet has gone, will it not, Esther? And, forgive me if I'm speaking out of turn, but might you not soon have some interesting news of your own?"

Esther hardly knew how to answer. Her young cousin was no fool, and Charlotte would not easily be bamboozled. "I see you think George and I have reached an understanding. You are mistaken. While I hope we each value the other's friendship, there is no question of marriage between us."

"What a slow-top he is. I would never have thought it. In fact, I know it not to be the case. He told me weeks ago that he regretted not declaring himself before your illness. Be assured, if he hasn't spoken yet, he certainly will soon."

Esther, not knowing what else to say, replied repressively, "I have no expectation of him doing so," and turning the subject asked Charlotte what she planned to do following her sister's departure. Then she wished that she had not done so, so shocked was she by her response.

"I shall become a merry widow, my dear, attending any number of functions during the season and visiting my friends in the country at every opportunity. You must not think I shall be lonely when you're both gone." This was said with a bravado which Charlotte did not feel, but it seemed Esther was convinced.

"But I shall not be leaving you, Charlotte. I wouldn't hear of you living on your own."

"Nonsense," said Charlotte and more she would not say on the subject.

The ladies entered with enthusiasm into the task of choosing Harriet's bride clothes. There was so much to be done in a short space of time. For her wedding dress Harriet had chosen a fine cotton dress in the French style, embroidered with satin thread. Its long-fitted sleeves were caught at the wrist with matching stitches which were repeated in the short train.

On the morning of Harriet's wedding, Esther clasped her mother's pearls around her neck and Charlotte stood facing her sister, holding her hands at arm's length. "You look so beautiful. A vision in ivory. You will be happy, I know. You will ride around the estate and engage with all your tenants. You will get smudges on your dress when the new lambs are born, for you will not be able to resist kneeling and helping. And everyone will love you, as we love you."

Esther, moving from behind her cousin to face her, merely said in her straightforward way, "Your mother would have been so proud," but there were tears in her eyes. How different this was from Charlotte's wedding only eighteen months before. This bride went eagerly and willingly to her new husband, her future bright before her.

"She seems to have blossomed these past months, don't you think?" Charlotte asked Esther, as Harriet said her goodbyes to the staff who had taken such good care of her. "It's as if she is ready to take this step and welcomes it with all her heart."

"Yes, she is looking forward to taking her place in her new home and I believe she cannot wait to get her hands dirty."

"I think Quentin has no idea what an asset she will prove to be, for she was always making suggestions for improvement when she rode around with me at Stapleton and she was much younger then."

"You've heard no more from your father?"

"Nothing." Sir Archibald had written the week previously to say that he was indisposed and would be unable to attend the wedding. "I can't understand him. His own daughter!" Charlotte said with frustration in her voice.

"Don't distress yourself. I don't believe she minds very much. She will be more comfortable if he is absent."

"I feel sure you are right. She needs only truly loving support, and you have given her that since she was a small child."

"I wish I could see you as happy, my dear. Your marriage was so unfortunate."

Charlotte did not deny it but merely commented, "Fewer than two years is such a small space in a lifetime. I shall come about, don't you worry. My dearest wish now is to see you as happy as Harriet. Then I shall be content. There is so much I wish to do. Do not imagine me sitting with my embroidery on my knees as I did while in mourning. There is a whole world out there, and I am ready to embrace it."

Despite Charlotte's optimistic tone, Esther felt a deep sadness within her, for it seemed Charlotte had turned her back on any thoughts of marrying for love. However, she quashed her instinctive protest and countered with a typical comment. "Just as well," she said, "for you never did learn how to set a stitch neatly."

The autumn sunshine streamed through the church windows and threw shafts of light onto the couple who stood facing the altar. The dust that danced in its rays was like confetti scattering its good wishes upon them. Once more assuming the mantle of guardian, Gresham had been given the honour of escorting the bride down the aisle and there was an expectant hush as people waited for Harriet and Quentin to exchange their vows. The couple took their parts in the ancient ceremony, speaking clearly and joyfully. Finally, the pronouncement came that they were man and wife, and there was a buzz as those present rose and moved to congratulate them.

"Are your fears at an end?"

Charlotte looked up to see Gresham standing at her side. She did not pretend to misunderstand him. "Oh no, I never feared it was wrong. Only that it was too soon. But look at her. Is she not a beautiful bride?" Gresham smiled and agreed.

They followed the rest from the church to St James's Square for the wedding breakfast. Charlotte reflected how very different Harriet's wedding was to her own. Here was only delight. This bride was joyful at the prospect of her new life and Charlotte was filled with happiness for her. When the time came for the bride and groom to leave, Harriet turned to embrace her sister before being helped into the carriage by her husband. They were to travel directly to Cranleigh. "With so much to do Quentin and I cannot wait to be started, but we will return to town as soon as can be, for I shall miss you dreadfully."

"Make sure you write first to establish that I am still here. I have plans of my own which will take me out of London," Charlotte teased. She did not elaborate, but though she did not wish to go she felt she must return to Stapleton to see what was ailing her father. As she waved the couple away, Gresham stood again at her side.

"I hope by that you mean you are to visit my mother, for she bade me expressly to remind you of your promise."

"How very kind of her. Indeed, if it will not tax her too much, I should be delighted. I spoke the truth just now, though. You will have noticed, I am sure, that my father is not here today. He wrote that he was ill and I would think less of myself if I did not try to discover what is amiss."

"Does your cousin go with you?"

"Oh no, she would not wish to return to Stapleton, I'm sure."

"May I then offer you my escort?"

Charlotte was taken aback and could not think how to respond. This chivalrous offer went beyond the familial duty he had so frequently asserted. She was strongly tempted to accept. She would enjoy both his company and his protection, but this was one journey she felt she must undertake alone. She placed little faith in her father's professed reason for not attending his daughter's wedding and felt, if she must confront him, she would prefer to do so in private. "That is kind of you, but I fear I must decline. May I write to the Duchess later, telling her when I am at leisure to visit?"

"Of course. And do, if you would like, bring your cousin with you to Gresham Hall."

"Thank you. I am not sure what her plans are, but I will certainly ask her. Goodbye, Your Grace. Please give my regards to your mother."

Gresham took her proffered hand. "Goodbye, Lady Cranleigh. I hope we shall meet again soon."

CHAPTER THIRTEEN

Naturally, Charlotte met with a good deal of resistance from Esther when told of her cousin's plan to return, for a while at least, to Stapleton. Only Harriet could have been equally aware of how little she wished to go, and Esther could not at first accept that Charlotte intended to travel unaccompanied.

"Bella goes with me, and Sam Coachman. My groom also. I need no other chaperone. Stay here, please, for such a visit will only distress you. Besides, poor Mr Harvey would go into a decline if you were to leave town now," Charlotte said teasingly.

Esther allowed herself to be persuaded for several reasons. Charlotte was right, the visit would distress her. She had no desire ever to return to Stapleton. She could see that her presence would be an anxiety rather than a help to Charlotte. And there was no denying she did not wish to leave London and, with it, George Harvey. Charlotte's encouragement of the courtship and her calm assumption that the marriage was a *fait accompli* had had their effect. Esther had come to appreciate that sheer strength of character would carry her dear girl through whatever the future might hold. That Charlotte would be more comfortable if her cousin continued to live with her was indisputable. But she continued to reiterate that she would not allow Esther to sacrifice her own happiness for that reason. Esther realised with a light heart that if George should renew his proposal, she would happily accept. Modest enough not to inform him of her change of mind, she could only hope that if she dropped a hint or two he would once again ask for her hand in marriage.

"You will write to me?"

"Of course, and I shall depend upon you to keep me informed of what goes on here in town while I am away."

Esther waved as the coach pulled away, but she would have been less content had she seen the smile fade from Charlotte's face as she sank back against the cushions. This was one journey she was not looking forward to. Her only consolation was that, ridden by her groom, Bess trotted beside the barouche. She hoped that at Stapleton they would have ample opportunity to shake off their fidgets.

It was a tedious journey into Hertfordshire, which did nothing to lighten Charlotte's frame of mind. However, as familiar landmarks came into view, she began to look forward to seeing her childhood home again. If nothing else, it at least held fond memories of her mother.

"And I will be happy to see our tenants again, for there is no doubt I have missed those times riding about the estate and meeting with them," she remarked to Bella, before subsiding again into silence as she realised they were no longer her tenants.

The light was fading as they reached Stapleton, and Charlotte went first to her room before seeking out her father, who had not come out to welcome her upon her arrival.

"I am delighted Jane has lit a fire. The evenings are beginning to turn quite chilly. It seems no time at all since we were complaining of the heat. Do please unpack my things and we can be comfortable again."

"Yes, my lady, and then, if you please, I shall go and look for Jane. It will be nice to see her again."

"I think she has not yet forgiven me for taking you with me to London, Bella, but I could not have done without you."

Bella turned pink with pleasure as Charlotte left the room and went in search of her parent. She found him in his library, but he was not studying any of the many volumes that adorned its walls. More, he was in a brown study of his own. Thinking this was not a good time, Charlotte retreated, hoping he might be in better frame when she confronted him later at dinner.

"I have been wondering, Papa, what was the nature of your indisposition that you were unable to attend Harriet's wedding," Charlotte said when the first course had been removed and she felt enough time had passed for her to broach the subject. "I hope you were not unwell for long?"

"I fear it is permanent," he replied abruptly.

"You've called the doctor?" she asked, worried now that he did indeed have some dreadful disease.

"There's nothing wrong with my health," he retorted. "Damnit, you ask too many questions."

Charlotte took a deep breath, as much to restrain her temper as to decide what to say next. "I have come expressly to see you, for I felt nothing short of serious illness could keep you from your daughter's wedding. I take it that was not the case."

He cast her a fulminating look. "It's none of your business, but I have been rusticating."

"I beg your pardon?"

"Keeping out of harm's way. If you must have it, Charlotte, I am seriously in debt. I have obligations I am unable to fulfil."

"But surely, last year, when Ernest…?"

"All gone. And now I don't know how I am to come about. It may be that I shall have to sell Stapleton," he said, throwing back a glass of the wine defiantly. He had already drunk far too much.

"Sell Stapleton!" Charlotte hadn't thought her father any longer had the power to surprise her, but this was something quite unexpected. He may have been a careless landlord, but the estate had been in his family for generations and she could not believe that he could bear to part with it. "Surely not! There must be another way."

"If there is, I don't know of it. Now stop chattering, girl, and let me finish my dinner in peace." Whereupon he poured himself another glass of wine and not another word was to be had from him for the rest of the evening.

Charlotte remained at the table for as long as she must but excused herself at the first opportunity. Her mind was in turmoil. Her marriage had all been for nothing. She had never felt more disgusted by her parent.

The following day she had breakfasted and was in the stables before her father could put in an appearance. To face him over the dinner table had been unpleasant enough, and her resolve was not sufficient to question him again before she had enjoyed a good gallop. She could feel Bess's excitement as she was being saddled up.

Just the sound of her hooves as she danced impatiently was all it took to lighten Charlotte's heart. She sent up a silent prayer of thanks to the Duchess of Gresham and resolved to do what she could to demonstrate her appreciation.

Some while later she reined in to a walk and it was only then that she noticed how neglected her surroundings appeared. This was shock enough in itself, but as she visited some of the tenants it became obvious that, wherever her father had invested the funds he had received from Ernest, it had certainly not been in his land.

"How lovely to see you again, Adam. I have been away far too long, it seems," she said to one man who stood respectfully with his hat in hand.

"Well, miss, I mean your Ladyship, there's no doubt things aren't the same as when you was in charge."

"But what of the steward? I cannot believe he would stand by and see things neglected in this way?"

"Mr Ludlow does what he can, your Ladyship, but his hands is tied."

"You are well enough acquainted with me to know that I like the word straight. Am I to understand that insufficient investment has been made available to run your farm as it was previously?"

"That's right."

"And will I find the same situation as I ride the estate?"

"You will, your Ladyship."

"Thank you for being so frank with me, Adam. I will be as frank with you. I don't know what can be done. I don't know if anything *can* be done. But I will do my best to discover what has happened here. I'm not sure how long my visit will be, but rest assured I will come and see you again before I leave."

"Thank you kindly, Miss Charlotte — I mean, your Ladyship. And welcome home."

To Charlotte, though, it no longer seemed like home.

"This new husband of Harriet's, is he fairly flush in the pocket, do you know?" Sir Archibald asked Charlotte at the dinner table.

"To what end would you ask me such a question? Have you no scruples? Isn't it enough that you have frittered away the funds that Ernest gave you? Do you now propose to apply to Mr Peacock as well?"

Charlotte was quite disgusted with her parent and barely knew how to maintain a civil front. He had explained that, in an attempt to capitalise on what he termed his windfall upon her marriage, he had endeavoured to increase the amount by speculating on the horses. He'd had indifferent luck, but disaster had really struck when he'd begun playing deep at the card table to try to recoup his losses. None of the money intended for Stapleton had found its way into the fabric of the building or the lands which surrounded it.

Charlotte would have remonstrated with him, but she realised his spirit was broken. Recrimination would do nothing to solve the problem.

"You will do no such thing," she said firmly, when it was obvious that he really did intend to apply to Quentin for money. "I will remain for a while and work with Ludlow to see what can be done to put things to rights with your tenants. I suggest you shut up most of the house and just maintain an apartment to meet your requirements. To my knowledge, you no longer entertain. You rarely use most of the rooms, so it cannot make a difference to you."

"How dare you speak to me in that manner!" her father shouted at her. "You will show me some respect while you are under this roof."

"You have killed any respect I had for you, and you no longer have the power to frighten me. I would not choose to remain here, but I fear there is no other way. Or do you really want to sell the home that has been passed down to you through generations of your family?" she asked reproachfully.

He subsided immediately, as is the way with bullies. "Do what you will. I no longer care."

It was obvious to Charlotte that regrettably she would be unable to undertake her visit to Gresham Hall as soon as she had hoped. She would make her apologies to the Duchess and write to Harriet and Esther to the effect that they should direct any future correspondence, for the time being at least, to Stapleton.

Charlotte received a reply from Esther.

Dearest Charlotte,

I know that you will not be surprised to learn of my news but I have been a little less than truthful with you. George, Mr Harvey I mean, has renewed his offer for my hand that I had earlier denied. I am happier than I can say. There are, however, a number of things which need resolving before we can take such a step. Harriet and Quentin are now settled at Cranleigh, and upon my marriage I would move to Mr Harvey's family home, for you know, none better, that it is in the country I am most happy. Our wedding will be a small affair, but I would not consider going ahead without your support. Are you able to return to London for some short period to come to the ceremony? Also, what would you have me do with the town house? Shall I arrange for it be closed up? Are you fixed at Stapleton for the foreseeable future?

Charlotte paused in her perusal of Esther's letter. She had been at Stapleton for some weeks now. There were signs of improvement in the management of the estate, a rewarding achievement when there was so little money available. But her determination and energy had instilled an enthusiasm in the tenants, and with hope in their hearts once more they had to a man and woman renewed their efforts. While Miss Charlotte was at the helm, they could not despair. She might be a Countess now but she did not disdain to get her hands dirty and was full of sound advice.

The house still remained closed up apart from the few rooms that were in daily use. Stapleton had been operating for a long time with a minimum number servants, some having remained only out of a perceived loyalty to the late Lady Willoughby. Others had been laid off. Her father had gone, she knew not where, nor much did she care.

She would herself return to the capital, for Esther's wedding and to put the house in St James's Square in order. If she was to succeed in restoring the estate to a footing whereby it could function without being broken up or sold, she would have to stay at least through the winter. She reflected how saddened Esther would be were she now to see the kitchen garden. Its management had always been in her capable hands but, though Charlotte was doing her best, little had been done to maintain it and there would be nothing like the variety of vegetables and herbs as in previous years. There were neither the funds nor the time.

She returned to her letter.

The season is well under way and I regret that you are missing some agreeable parties. You are asked for everywhere. I heard that your father had returned to town but is gone again, to stay with friends, I believe. I know from your letters that you are doing what you can with the land, but I fear you must be feeling lonely. I will come to you for a while if you would like, before the wedding. George says he can spare me, knowing I am to be his for the future. Or, if you are to come to St James's, advise me of your arrival so I can have the fire lit in your bedchamber to welcome you home. You cannot know how much I miss you.

Esther

Charlotte put pen to paper immediately.

Dearest Esther,

You are right of course, but the lack of surprise in no way diminishes my joy at your news. Of course I shall come to London. How could you imagine otherwise? While I fear I must put my own plans on hold for some time, until my work here is done, I will make haste to join you for a few weeks. I know you have impeccable taste, but I should be desolated should you choose your trousseau without me. This letter will, I trust, reach you before I do, but only in time for you to anticipate my arrival. I will follow hard upon it and be with you as soon as ever I can. Does Harriet come to your wedding? Do not reply. I shall be with you before your letter could reach me and I shall receive your answer in person.

With love, Charlotte.

Charlotte immediately began packing for her return to London, pausing only to interview Ludlow and assure him she would soon be back to continue their collective efforts to rescue the estate.

The journey to town was if anything more tiresome than had been that into the country. Bess and her groom remained at Stapleton, and consequently Charlotte would not even be able to enjoy the pleasure of her daily rides, but she felt it impractical to take the mare with her. She would be well-cared-for where she was. It would be Charlotte, not Bess, who was the loser.

"Come inside quickly, my dear," Esther said upon Charlotte's arrival. "It has turned quite cold, and you must be tired. A fire has been lit in the morning room and I have had dinner set back in anticipation of your arrival."

Charlotte felt almost like a child again as Esther took her under her wing. She let go a sigh of relief and allowed herself to be led into the house. Pausing only to remove her gloves and bonnet, she followed where her cousin led. "So tell me all that you could not in your last letter. Does Harriet come? When are you to be married?"

"Yes, she and Mr Peacock will join us in just above a week from now and the wedding is to take place only four days after that. George is anxious to make me his bride before I am able to change my mind."

Charlotte looked up, somewhat surprised. "Change your mind?"

"No, I spoke in jest, but we are both of the opinion that at our age the sooner the thing is done, and with the minimum of fuss, the better. We shall give the dressmaker a fine task, though, won't we? Do not think you will be permitted to rest up tomorrow, for I have already arranged for a visit. We shall look at patterns, though I have sketched some ideas which I will show you presently. Then we will need to choose fabrics. Harriet brings something with her that she has had made up in Milsom Street. You remember, do you not, how keen she was to return there."

Charlotte was swept up in Esther's excitement and they spent the next few days in a whirl of activity.

On the fifth evening after her return, they went to Almack's Assembly Rooms. Mr Harvey came soon to claim Esther, and Charlotte found herself greeted by many of her acquaintances, who berated her for staying away for so long. Among them was Viscount Roxburgh. It was all she could do to be polite to him, but his behaviour was as if what had passed between them on their last meeting had never occurred. She responded in kind, thinking this was the best way and hoping that episode could be put behind her forever.

Cosmo Fortescue, coming next to demand her attention, drew her away and they were soon joined by the Duke of Gresham. Unaccountably she felt lighter of spirit.

"My mother was disappointed that you found it necessary to put off your visit," Gresham said. "She hopes, I know, that the delay will not be of long duration."

Charlotte was conscious of a desire to unburden herself to him as she no longer could to Esther or Harriet. "I am only come to town for my cousin's wedding. There is much to do at Stapleton, and I fear I must return for some weeks before I am able to pick up the reins again."

"It is to be hoped you will have the whip hand before long."

"Indeed I hope so, for you know it was not my wish to return to Hertfordshire."

"Is your father well?"

"I cannot say, for he left some weeks ago. I am unaware of his present whereabouts."

"So you are once again in charge at Stapleton?"

"By default only. I hope to relinquish that role as soon as may be. In the meantime, though, I must see it through."

Gresham looked thoughtful and Cosmo asked, "Is there none to aid you? It seems a huge burden for you to bear alone."

"But one I am accustomed to, my friend, for it was my role before I married the Earl. It isn't the magnitude of the task that daunts me but the fact that it isn't where I would wish to be."

"You know, and I am sure I speak also for Fortescue, that you may call upon us at any time."

Charlotte was almost overset by these two good friends on whom she recognised she was beginning to lean more than she could wish. She would not for the world impose upon Cosmo, because she was aware of his declared feelings for her and anything that might be perceived as tying her closer to him seemed in her eyes to be unfair. Gresham, however, had many times expressed his willingness to act as her titular guardian and she felt she would not be too proud to apply to him for advice, should the need arise. She found the thought gave her comfort.

"It is my intention to go to Drury Lane tomorrow evening, where I have a box at the Theatre Royal. If you are not yet engaged, would you care to join me?" Cosmo asked her.

"I am not, and I should be delighted, Cosmo. It is my wish to cram in as many delights as I am able before returning to the country. Oh, but Harriet and Quentin arrive tomorrow. I could not leave them on their first day."

"Then, if they are not too fatigued by the journey, do beg them to come as well."

"I shall do so and, if they are too tired to go out, they will not want me to be paying them a visit either. You must know that Quentin has purchased a house in town for Harriet of which they are both inordinately proud, and this will be their first opportunity to stay there. They may wish to dine at home, I cannot say. So I shall say yes, thank you, on my own behalf and send word to you tomorrow if they are to make up the party."

"Excellent. How about you, Gresham? Care to come?" Cosmo said, turning to his friend.

"I too would have been delighted, but I am already pledged to join Maria Stanford. Perhaps we might all meet up during the interval."

Charlotte felt a momentary disappointment but put it quickly aside. She spent much of the evening in a high state of contentment, the encounter with Roxburgh having been the only thing to mar her enjoyment. She set this determinedly aside and later told Esther that she would be happy to divide her time between the urban and the rural. She felt blessed to be able to enjoy the freedom that being at Stapleton afforded her, but her return to London had highlighted how much she missed her friends. Being solitary, she found, did not suit her at all.

Shortly before the evening ended, Charlotte was surprised when Viscount Roxburgh approached her again.

"My dear Lady Cranleigh. It is fortuitous that you are again in London, as there is something which I wish to speak to you about. May I call upon you one morning next week, after your cousin's wedding?"

"You can have nothing to say to me, Lord Roxburgh, that cannot be said here and now."

"You are wrong, my dear. I have something of importance that you most certainly would not wish to have discussed in public. It concerns your father, and I would urge you to agree to see me."

How dared he call her 'my dear'! Was there was a hint of menace in his voice? The man had displayed the power to make her wary ever since she'd known him. But she retained enough filial concern to be worried by his sinister reference to her father. She didn't know where he was and sensed, if Roxburgh did, that he might be in trouble. She therefore consented to receive the Viscount when he called.

He moved away immediately, but he had cast a cloud which she was unable to dispel for the remainder of the evening.

CHAPTER FOURTEEN

"We have stopped outside only that I may come and see you straight away, for I could not bear to wait a moment longer," Harriet said the following afternoon, hugging Charlotte and Esther in turn. "Quentin waits in the square and we must make haste. It has been a long journey, and there is so much to attend to. The horses need to be stabled … yes, of course they must come first," she retorted, seeing the smile on her sister's face. "And I don't see why you are laughing. It is only what you taught me, after all."

"And after the horses?"

"Well, naturally it will take us some time to get settled in. I shall have no idea where to put things. I cannot believe you are to be married in just four days, Esther," she said, taking her cousin's hands in her own, the excitement spilling from her. "Will you both forgive me if I don't call again until tomorrow? We should like to spend our first evening alone," she added, a little shyly. Soon after she left like the whirlwind of a girl they were used to, and Charlotte sent word to Cosmo Fortescue that Mr and Mrs Peacock would not be joining them in Drury Lane.

Esther, though she too had been invited, chose to remain in St James's Square for the evening. She still had much to do and, with Bella's help, they made final decisions on what she was to take with her to her new home and what would be packed and stored to be reviewed at a later date.

On being shown to Cosmo's box and exchanging greetings with others of his guests, a couple she already knew and another with whom she was unacquainted, Charlotte took her place and was silent for a few moments as she gazed around. Then a hush fell upon the auditorium as the performance began. In all her twenty-two years, this was only her second visit to the theatre. At Stapleton there had been none in the vicinity.

As a well-educated young lady she was naturally familiar with Shakespeare's plays, but it was only that first occasion when she had gone with Ernest that had prepared her for the personification of characters who had previously been known to her only in the pages of a book. She was enraptured.

"I see you are pleased with what you have seen," Cosmo said as the interval began. "I have addressed you twice before managing to gain your attention," he said with a smile.

"I cannot thank you enough. I feel quite breathless. Please forgive me, I had no intention of being impolite."

"Nor were you. Come now to the back of the box, where there are some refreshments. The Radcliffs have gone to see friends and will return shortly. Let us help ourselves before we too receive visitors as I am sure we shall, having seen several people looking in your direction when first you arrived."

"Oh yes. Did the Duke not say we might meet during the evening?"

"He did, but it would seem he is in close conversation with Maria Stanford and is unable to get away," he said, pointing to one of the boxes on the opposite side of the theatre just as Maria looked up and acknowledged them with a wave. "Ah, Hector, perhaps I can offer you something from this plate. It is not immediately recognisable to me, but I am assured it is delicious," he said, turning to Mr Ruthin, who was also his guest.

"Delighted, dear boy. Never been known to turn something down just because it looked a bit odd." Then, realising the implication, "Not that I'm suggesting it is odd."

"Don't worry, Hector. I had taken no offence. Lady Cranleigh has just been asking how your new horse is coming along."

Charlotte shot a look of reproach at Cosmo, at the same time being overcome by a fit of coughing as she recalled his rather low opinion of his friend's ability to judge a horse. "Please excuse me. Something has caught in my throat."

She recovered well enough but had to endure Mr Ruthin's raptures until it was time for the curtain to rise again. She inwardly vowed her revenge on Cosmo and told him so at the end of the evening when she had the opportunity for a quiet word.

"I'm sorry, Charlotte, but the temptation was irresistible. I deserve whatever punishment you choose to impose upon me."

"How ungallant you are, dear friend, when you know well that I am so obliged to you for such a wonderful evening and must not allow myself to say what I'm thinking. I expect you know what it is, though."

"Indeed, and if I may be permitted to visit you in St James's Square after your cousin's wedding you may rake me over the coals as much as you desire."

"I should be delighted to see you, for that or any reason. Thank you so much for inviting me. It was a truly marvellous experience."

If Charlotte had been disappointed that Gresham had not attended Mr Fortescue's box at the theatre, it wasn't something she acknowledged to herself. The wedding of Esther to

George Harvey was a very small affair with just a handful of guests, and all of those being family members of either the bride or groom. It seemed to Charlotte no time at all since she had attended the bridal ceremony of her sister. Now the two people dearest to her in all the world were gone.

The following morning, Charlotte found herself alone in St James's Square for the first time since her own marriage to Ernest. It was a strange sensation, almost akin to fear, but before she had time to analyse how she felt she became aware that there was someone at the door and the footman was announcing a visitor. Her heart sank, for her first instinct was to believe Lord Roxburgh was paying the promised call. Summoning what resolution she could, she stood to greet her guest, but it was Gresham, not Roxburgh, who was ushered into the morning room.

"I trust I do not impose. It seemed to me that you might have need of a friend this morning."

It was with difficulty that Charlotte held back her tears. She had willed herself to be strong, but these words of sympathy put her severely out of countenance. She was about to protest that all was well, but Gresham was no fool. He moved towards her and took her hands.

"You are upset. And pale. Will you sit down? Would you prefer that I leave?"

"No, Your Grace, you are very welcome. But I was expecting someone else. A visitor I am not wishful of meeting."

"Can you not refuse to see them?"

"I fear not. I make no bones, for you have been a good friend and have offered your service should I need it."

"You need it now?"

Charlotte wasn't quite sure how to proceed. Aware as she was of the antipathy that Gresham and Roxburgh had each for the other, she felt it prudent to tread carefully. But she urgently wanted to confide in someone. Not Esther, who was even now on her honeymoon, nor Harriet, who was only in town for a few days. It would be unkind to spoil her visit by burdening her sister with her own troubles.

"Not exactly, but might I at least share my misgivings with you, if you will allow me to do so?"

"Of course. I am your servant. You know that. Who is it that has disturbed you so?"

"It is Roxburgh."

"What!"

"He has asked, no, *demanded* that I receive him, for he tells me he has something of importance to tell me which concerns my father."

Gresham began pacing the room but came to a halt in front of her. "You know that there is no love lost between myself and that gentleman. If he plagues you in any way, he will have me to answer to."

His agitation in some way prompted Charlotte to put things in perspective, and she began to think she was perhaps making too much of the situation. She made haste to reassure him that she was well able to deal with the interview but that her concern was for her parent. She begged him to think no more about it.

"You will permit me, I hope, to call each day to see how you go on. I am fixed in town for some time. If you need me, you have only to send word. I am more honoured than I can say that you have taken me into your confidence." The passion had gone out of his voice but the intensity was still there. "You can rest assured that I shall keep a watchful eye over you, Lady Cranleigh. You may well have experienced marriage and widowhood in your short life, but you are not completely awake on every suit yet, you know," he added, and there was kindness in his words. "I shall leave you now, but I will return tomorrow."

And he was gone. Charlotte could at last allow her pent-up tears to flow.

The anticipated visit came the following morning and was in a way a relief for Charlotte, who had been in a state of apprehension for two days.

"My dear Lady Cranleigh, it is a delight to see you," Lord Roxburgh said, bowing over her hand in that manner she found so disturbing.

"Do please be seated, my Lord, and tell me what you know of my father."

"Ah, straight to the point. I like that directness in you."

Charlotte cared not at all that he liked or disliked her manner. She was anxious to learn what she could and get this over with as soon as possible, but she was astounded at what he said next.

"Let me then also be direct. I ask you again, Charlotte, to be my wife."

There was a pause as she swallowed hard before saying, "Did I not request when you came to Cranleigh that you never speak to me of this again? Your coming here today was, I understood, to give me news of my parent."

"Your father, I understand, has withdrawn from society for the time being. I believe, no, I am sure, that I am the cause of his present retirement."

His tone was unemotional. Charlotte folded her hands in her lap and waited.

"You will know of his fondness for cards. He did me the honour of playing with me several times. The luck was not with him."

She went cold, remembering the story of Gresham's cousin.

"It seems that he hazarded more than was wise. More than he could repay. I have his promissory notes with me now. Say you will be mine and I shall tear them up here and now and throw them on this fire."

"You would *blackmail* me!"

"A nasty word, my dear. I would show you how you can be instrumental in preventing your family name being hauled through the mud."

Charlotte was consumed with anger. The fear that she had barely allowed herself to feel evaporated in a wave of heat that brought her to her feet. "You will leave now. I have told you before that I cannot return your regard, but that you should stoop so low sickens me. I would prefer in future, should we meet in public, that you will not claim acquaintanceship with me, for I shall most surely disregard you."

Roxburgh too was on his feet and moved towards her, but Charlotte had already rung the bell and the footman knocked and entered, leaving the Viscount with no choice but to take his leave.

"I hope you find your father well when next you see him, my Lady," he said silkily, with an ironic bow, but there was no doubt in her mind of the threat that lay behind his words.

True to his promise, Gresham arrived not half an hour after Roxburgh's departure. Charlotte was still pacing up and down when he was shown into the morning room, her fury all the worse for having no physical outlet. Had she brought Bess with her to London, nothing would have suited her better than

144

a good canter in the park. She came to a halt and returned the pressure on the hand that took hers.

"He has called. You have no need to tell me, for it shows in your countenance. Come, sit down and tell me, if you will, what has occurred here."

Had her feelings been more under control she might have kept her own counsel, but Charlotte was still in a rage and the whole story came tumbling out. "Viscount Roxburgh has done me the honour of asking me to be his wife," she said, her voice full of sarcasm. "It would seem he is holding my father's vowels but will be happy to tear them up, put them on this very fire," she said, pointing at it as if it was in itself offensive, "would I but consent to his proposal! How could he think I would? What kind of a woman does he believe me to be? Oh, I cannot bear it," she asserted, resuming her pacing.

"It does not surprise me that a man of his stamp would resort to such tactics, despicable as they are. I will consider how you may thwart him. But you are angry and distressed, and justly so. How would it be if I have two of my horses brought round and we go for a ride? I cannot promise you a mount such as Bess, but I often find when I am stressed that it is a relief to be on the move."

Charlotte's look of gratitude showed her appreciation. "That would be kind of you indeed and just what I need. I had only just been thinking before you came of my regret that I do not have Bess with me in London. I will get changed immediately and be ready when you return."

As they walked their horses to the park, Charlotte was able to get a feel for the mount Gresham had chosen for her. It was true she was no Bess, but she had spirit and responded well to her rider's commands. Once through the gates they were able to let the reins go and Charlotte was so lost in the pleasure of the activity that she was even unaware that Gresham was matching her stride for stride. When they reined in to a walk she was able to say in all honesty, "Oh, I feel so much calmer. Thank you, Your Grace. You could not have suggested anything better just at the moment."

Gresham looked at her and smiled somewhat ruefully. "You are used, I know, to calling Mr Fortescue by his given name, but you have never yet used mine. We are friends, are we not? It would give me much pleasure if you could do the same, for I feel, whenever you call me Your Grace, that I have done something to cause you displeasure."

"Oh no, not that. Well, not often anyway," she said with an innate honesty. She blushed a little too, was aware of it and hoped he would put it down to the exhilaration of the ride.

"And?"

"And I shall be honoured to call you Sebastian, except at such times as you have caused me displeasure," she added as a rider, but with a smile.

"Then I shall endeavour not to cause you any."

CHAPTER FIFTEEN

Sebastian was putting his mind to trying to find a solution to Charlotte's problem. He couldn't stand by while a man of Roxburgh's sort behaved in a way that shamed his peers. To take advantage of Sir Archibald's age and predilections was unforgivable. He had seen Roxburgh play; he knew he was good. He also knew that Roxburgh would have been aware of Sir Archibald's straightened circumstances. A gentleman would have withdrawn. Roxburgh was not a gentleman!

More to the point, Sebastian admitted to himself that his guardianship of Lady Cranleigh, undertaken at first out of recognition of some tenuous family obligation, had become more personal. He would do much to shield her from pain. She had been forced into an arranged marriage and had become the stronger for it, and he had viewed with approval that she conducted herself in society after an unfortunate start with not just the dignity of her position but with a natural poise.

The fact that Charlotte had rejected Roxburgh might further endanger her father and the future of her family home.

Sebastian decided to visit Charlotte again in the morning. He would, had he been able, have liked to have private conversation with her, but when he arrived in St James's Square the following day Mr and Mrs Peacock were before him.

"How lovely to see you, Your Grace. It seems an age since we were all together at Cranleigh," Harriet said very prettily. "Though you were at our wedding, I didn't have the pleasure of talking to you as much as I could have wished."

"Yes, it's good to see you, Gresham," Quentin said, shaking his friend by the hand. "We are looking forward to you coming to visit us in Wiltshire. You will be pleased, I think, with what we have done there."

Sebastian said all that was correct but he was surreptitiously watching Charlotte. She was still a little pale, but her spirits seemed raised by her sister's visit. He announced that he would be leaving London the next day for business at home. "I have had some thoughts since I spoke to you yesterday," he said. "I believe I may be able to resolve the problem we discussed."

This was all he was able to impart to her without arousing a curiosity in Harriet and Quentin that he knew she would not wish. With that she had to be content, and when he took his leave he pressed her hand firmly in the hope she would draw some reassurance from the gesture. Then he was gone.

Sebastian went straight away to see Roxburgh. The most pressing thing in his opinion was to get his hands on those notes. Experience had proved that Roxburgh was entirely unprincipled, and he would have no compunction, Sebastian was sure, in disgracing Charlotte, if only by association with her father, now that he had been unable to force her into marriage. It was a matter of urgency that the means to do so was removed from him. Sebastian determined to gain possession of Sir Archibald's vowels. There was a look of astonishment on Roxburgh's face when, after two vain attempts, Sebastian finally ran him to ground in his club.

"I would have speech with you in private, my Lord," said Sebastian without preamble.

Roxburgh rose from his chair and the two found a quiet room where they would not be disturbed. When Sebastian outlined his proposition, Roxburgh laughed in his face. "You would not, I know, expect me to relinquish them at their face value, I am sure," he said, the sneer marring his otherwise handsome features.

"If you were a gentleman, yes, I would. However, you are correct and I will give you a quarter as much again of their worth. Do not delude yourself. This is my one and only offer. Take it or leave it."

"Very well. Naturally I do not carry the chits with me. Come with me to my chambers and I shall hand them over to you."

Roxburgh and Gresham completed their transaction and took their leave of each other. Only force of will prevented Sebastian from then wiping his hands on his breeches, so dirty did he feel.

Sebastian's next object was to track down Sir Archibald to inform him that he was himself now the holder of the promissory notes and, with a plan in mind, to lay his proposition before him. There was no guarantee that he would find his quarry at first attempt, but there was a good chance he would be at Barrington's hunting lodge in the shires, so Sebastian journeyed north, going over in his head the plans he had for his various enterprises. While he had begun at Gresham Hall in a fairly modest way prior to Ernest's demise, the proposed undertaking at Stapleton meant that what had started as a small seed had grown out of all expectation. Barrington was a little surprised at his arrival for, though acquainted, they were not close friends, but the older man took it in good part and invited him to stay.

"We've had some good sport this last week. You are very welcome to join us."

"Thank you, you are very kind. I will not remain above a day or two, but I was in the area and had heard so much of your place here I thought to take the liberty of paying a visit," he said with the disarming smile with which those of his close circle were so familiar.

"Good, then you shall join us tomorrow. I have one or two mounts I am sure would be up to your weight. Come and meet the rest."

He took Sebastian into a room where were assembled some half a dozen gentleman, and Sebastian was relieved to note that Sir Archibald was one of their number. Most of the people were known to him in some degree or other, and he passed a very convivial evening hearing anecdotes of their recent activities. He had no opportunity that night to separate his quarry from the rest but managed to take Charlotte's father aside when they returned from the hunt the following day. Not one to beat about the bush, he came straight to the point.

"It has come to my attention, Sir Archibald, that you are desirous of making some changes at Stapleton and I wondered if we might perhaps be of use to each other. It has become a hobby of mine to breed horses, and I am aware you are a clipping rider and like the animals for their own sake. It occurred to me while I was casting around for somewhere to establish another stud that we might, the two of us, work together. Naturally, I could not be present all the time and have been looking to find one whom I could trust to oversee a project so close to my heart. So you see, sir, now that I have explained the matter to you, how convenient it would be for me to have another property on which I might raise my horses. Your reputation goes before you as a good judge and I would be grateful in the extreme if you would allow me to install such facilities as are necessary at Stapleton."

"You honour me, sir, but you are in the right of it. My cattle have always been my passion and I must say the idea appeals greatly. Yes, very greatly indeed. Let us shake hands on it, then."

Sebastian had handled the situation with all the tact of which he was capable, explaining that he held the other man's vowels but placing emphasis on the enterprise. Sir Archibald had no reason to question how the duke might have come by his knowledge. With Sebastian showing respect for the older man, Sir Archibald was able to feel that it was he doing Gresham a favour, rather than himself being rescued from an untenable situation.

"I hope we shall meet soon at Stapleton. It may be that my man of business, Mr Downing, will see you before I do. He will be in possession of all the plans and will familiarise you with them at the first opportunity."

"I shall look forward to making his acquaintance. I plan to return home in a week or two," Sir Archibald said, shaking Sebastian by the hand once more.

Sebastian could not much like him, but nor could he despise him. That his character was weak was already known, but he had handled a difficult conversation with dignity and that was to his credit. He left the next morning, well satisfied with the outcome.

The following week Charlotte was astonished, as she returned to Stapleton on foot across the front lawn, to see Sebastian's carriage sweeping up the drive. She was pleasantly surprised, for he had not advised her of his coming. Sebastian reined in as she waved at him.

"It's good to see you, Sebastian," she said, greeting him warmly. "Already I am missing the company of those in town, though I admit I have had little time to think of my own pleasures since I arrived."

Sebastian handed the reins to his groom with instructions to drive to the stables and walked together with Charlotte to the house. "You have much to do here, I understand."

"I do indeed, though how you could be aware I am at a loss to know."

Charlotte was a proud woman and Sebastian chose his words carefully. "You may remember I left London in rather a hurry. I said I had business to attend to and that was true. I also said I might have a solution to the problem you were so generous as to tell me about. You must know I have redeemed your father's vowels."

Charlotte halted in her tracks, looking as astonished as she felt. "But why?"

"Roxburgh is a dangerous man. I have hinted as much before. I felt they would be safer in my hands."

"Am I to understand, sir, that you still have them? You will know better than any other that Ernest's will was left in such a way as I am unable to discharge my father's debts."

"Yes."

"What would you have me do?" she said, her voice raised in agitation.

"Why, nothing. I have been to see your father. The matter has been settled. He is to return here shortly to manage a facility which I am planning to put in place. You already know what is being done at Cranleigh. I would wish a similar breeding programme to happen here."

"You cannot be serious! My father is not able to run such an enterprise!"

"Perhaps not, but Ludlow, with the help of my man of business, is well able to do so. Your father, I must tell you, is more than happy with the arrangement. He remains in his home and will be occupied with breeding horses. If you ask me, it will suit him very well."

"But I do not ask you!" she snapped. "How dare you behave in such a high-handed way? And without as much as a word to me? Do you think because of your wealth and position you are able to run people's lives for them?" They had by this time entered the house and moved into the library, an area Charlotte's father had retained the use of. "Forgive me, I must leave the room before I say something I shall regret."

She swept out furiously, leaving Sebastian unable to respond, but she returned almost immediately and stood in the doorway, taut with indignation, her lovely eyes flashing green fire.

"It is evident that I do not have the power to ask that you leave since my father has agreed to your suggestion, but I would request you have as little as possible to do with me for the duration of your visit."

And she was gone again.

Sebastian smiled ruefully, acknowledging to himself that he should have shared his plans with her. In his desire to resolve her difficulties he had rushed his fences. For the moment she had withdrawn her friendship. It remained to be seen whether he could win her round again, but the glimpse he had seen of her passionate nature dazzled him. She was magnificent!

Charlotte was in no frame of mind to sit with Sebastian that evening, leaving him to dine alone while she took her supper on a tray in her room. The atmosphere was still frosty when Sebastian left Stapleton the following day. He deemed it unwise to remain longer. This left Charlotte, once her anger had cooled, to reflect that perhaps she had over-reacted and to endure the frustration of being unable to tell him so. It had belatedly dawned that he had lifted a great weight from her shoulders. While she would never have shirked what she considered to be an obligation, coming back to Stapleton had been a burden. She could not do the job as she would wish without sufficient funds. She had cause (reluctantly) to be grateful to the man and had to admit she admired his scheme. And she had been extremely pleased to see him, at first … but this she would not properly acknowledge to herself, putting it down to her isolation at Stapleton.

As for Sebastian, nothing further could be done until plans were drawn up. He perceived that he had been a thorn in his hostess's side. Relations had not been as bad between them since he had visited her all those months ago in St James's Square, still suspicious of her.

Feeling unsettled, and unaware that Charlotte was experiencing similar emotions, he chose not to return home but journeyed instead into Wiltshire to see how Harriet and Quentin did. He remained for some days, taking great satisfaction in what had so far been achieved. Quentin was well-suited to the task in hand and in Harriet he had a willing and capable helper, visiting tenants and getting on good terms with the housekeeper.

Sebastian had several discussions with Ingram, who seemed to be revelling in the work. The estate had not been neglected during Ernest's time but the steward felt that standing idle and unoccupied for a year had caused it to lose some of its soul. For this Sebastian felt responsible and told the steward so quite frankly. While he had of course no need to explain himself to Ingram, he wanted him to know that he'd taken his time to consider what the best course of action might be. "I was never going to take up residence here. My own estates are extensive and I have enough to do there. Until this idea presented itself to me I am afraid there was little I could do, but I trust your master, were he able to see, would be proud of what is being done with his home."

"I have lived here from a boy, sir, and I can say with certainly that would be the case."

Sebastian received word that Sir Archibald had returned to Stapleton and so he returned to Hertfordshire, wondering what sort of reception he would receive from Charlotte. He was relieved to detect a softening in her attitude towards him. Conversation was made easier because her father was at his most ebullient. Sir Archibald had discussed the plans, in so far as they were established, with Ludlow and was vastly looking forward to a future where all responsibility was removed from his shoulders. That his estate would be put in order without any obligation to himself was just what he liked. He would, he knew, receive credit for all that was done, for Sebastian had assured him that none should know of their arrangement.

Charlotte, meanwhile, had taken up her old activities for the time being but the new plans meant that her presence, though welcomed by the tenants, was no longer necessary. Stapleton felt less like home to her than ever and although she had forgiven Sebastian, she could not help feeling slightly resentful. She resolved to leave and return to London. The decision cost her a pang, for neither Harriet nor Esther would be in St James's Square to welcome her.

"I will be leaving shortly, Father," she said at dinner one evening, addressing her parent while at the same time informing Sebastian of her intentions, which was her real purpose.

As ever, Sir Archibald was not overly interested in his daughter's movements and even less so now he no longer needed her. He asked, but only out of politeness, "You are returning to town?"

"Yes, that is what I mean to do."

"Forgive me, Lady Cranleigh, but if there is nothing urgent requiring your presence there, I am wondering if now might be a convenient time for you to pay a visit to my mother?" Sebastian asked.

Charlotte looked across the table at him, for a moment not quite sure what to do. She certainly had a desire to see the Duchess again. Coupled with this was a curiosity about Gresham Hall which could only be satisfied by seeing it. And it occurred to her that it would delay the day when she had to return to her empty house. Therefore, it was with a reasonable degree of warmth that she replied, "My plans are not fixed, Your Grace. If she is well enough to receive me, I should be delighted."

"Very well, then. It is lucky, is it not, that Bess is here at Stapleton, for I believe you had formed the intention of taking her when you visit my mother."

Charlotte's spirits were lifting with each moment. She realised she would be giving pleasure to the Duchess and this would in some way alleviate any obligation she might feel. "What a wonderful idea. I should like above all things to take Bess with me, if I may."

Both Charlotte and Sebastian were relieved to be on good terms again. It was consequently in high spirits that they set out for Sebastian's country seat. Charlotte would preferred to have ridden alongside him, but apart from the possible impropriety of this, conditions were grim and she thought it best to keep to the carriage with Bella for company. They were obliged to break their journey at an inn for one night, where

Sebastian engaged a private parlour and they dined with Bella in the role of chaperone.

"It is to be hoped during your stay that we may ride together," Sebastian said. "Sable and Bess are old friends, and it would give me great pleasure to show you where I grew up. There is much to see, so I trust you have no pressing need to return to London."

"No indeed," Charlotte replied. "I am greatly looking forward to seeing your estate. It will be interesting to compare it to Cranleigh and Stapleton, though it must be far larger."

Conversation flowed easily between them as Sebastian told Charlotte he had been to Wiltshire and was able to report on her sister and brother-in-law's wellbeing. "And already they are making their mark."

"Yes, I cannot imagine Harriet would be idle for long. It was her habit to accompany me around the estate when we were at Stapleton."

It was after Charlotte retired to her room that she took a letter from her reticule. It was from Harriet and had arrived shortly before they'd left Stapleton. Rather than hasten to read it, Charlotte had kept it back to enjoy at her leisure. She sat at the small table and moved the candle to throw as much light as possible onto the missive. It was full of information about the day-to-day life at Cranleigh and there was no doubt in her mind that Harriet was as happy as could be.

Mostly it's the boys that take up my time. You wouldn't believe what some of them have been through. Unimaginable cruelty and distress. But wait. You are not aware. I keep forgetting that none of these things was in place when we all stayed here together.

Boys? What boys? Charlotte wondered. *The Duke said nothing about boys!*

So many plans have been put forward and executed. It would seem that Gresham desires the estate to be put to good use as a tribute to Ernest, for else it would fall into disrepair. We are privileged to live here but be assured we are not idle, the Duke having entrusted the whole enterprise to Quentin. You may say that I would naturally favour him, and you would be right of course, but Quentin is doing a magnificent job in bringing to fruition the Duke's programme. The new stables are in a way to being built and there is to be a smithy and a tannery too. All manner of leather work connected with the horses will be undertaken. Oh, and there is talk of a coachworks as well. Then there are the gardens, and the animals … and, well, so much I do not know how to describe it all.

There are several boys here already, and there will be more when some of the work is finished. They are to be instructed in all sorts of useful occupations and, upon their leaving, others will take their place. It seems that there is a side to the Duke of which we had no suspicion. But you should see them, my darling. One poor specimen has scars covering his back where he has been so ill-treated and I feared he would not survive. There was barely any flesh covering his bones, but you would be amazed at what a few weeks in the country with proper food can do. He works in the kitchen. Yes, even there boys are being trained for some future occupation.

But what of you? Do you remain long at Stapleton? I cannot believe you are happy there and would be glad to learn of your return to London. You know without me saying that you are welcome here at any time. Perhaps you might come in the spring and we can once again venture into Bath and visit all those lovely shops in Milsom Street.

I received a delightful letter from Esther only last week. It seems that she and George are most happy in their marriage. I miss her dreadfully, as I do you, my dear sister. Write soon.

Yours affectionately, Harriet

"Well!" Charlotte said to the empty room. "It would seem that under his sometimes proud exterior the Duke is a charitable man." She folded the letter and put it back in her reticule. The light was not good enough for her to reply to Harriet immediately but she would do so as soon as she could after reaching Gresham Hall. She resolved to tell Sebastian nothing of this insight into his character. It seemed he was adept at hiding his light under a bushel, and it would be interesting to know if he meant to keep his philanthropy a secret forever.

CHAPTER SIXTEEN

The day was much advanced when Charlotte and Sebastian finally arrived at Gresham Hall. Charlotte was disappointed not to be able to have a clear picture of the imposing building, for such it was, as they approached from a drive that seemed at the time to be endless. There was moonlight enough on this crisp winter evening to guide their progress and Charlotte's first impression as she peered out of the window was of an establishment that stretched far to the left and right of her field of vision. She wondered if it was as deep as it was wide and was looking forward to learning more in the coming days.

Sebastian gave instructions for the unloading of the luggage and helped Charlotte down from the carriage. A young lad, Jim, Sebastian had called him, came rushing out to take Sable from Sebastian, before Charlotte and Sebastian walked into the house.

"I should like to take you to my mother straight away, if you are agreeable."

"Oh no. Please allow me to wash and change. I would be loath to greet the Duchess as I am."

"She would not mind in the least."

"Perhaps not, but I would," Charlotte said with a rueful smile. "I have been travelling for much of the day and am most certainly not fit to be presented."

"I see nothing wrong," he said, with a warm look that made the breath catch in her throat. Not wanting to question the cause, she allowed herself to be shown upstairs to her chamber. She was delighted to find it tastefully furnished, the drapes on the four-poster bed matching those that hung on the windows; an escritoire and chair placed to one side — at which she resolved to write to Esther, as well as Harriet at the first opportunity. A chaise longue was set at an angle by the window, the more to catch the light. All was in readiness for her arrival.

With an awestruck Bella to aid her Charlotte was soon descending the grand stairway to be met by a footman who guided her to the Duchess's sitting room. Here she was warmly welcomed, and introduced to Sophia, her Grace's companion.

"I am so delighted you could come, my dear," the Duchess said. "These cold winter days will be warmed for a while by the pleasure of your company. I hope you find your bedchamber comfortable."

"Indeed yes, Your Grace, I feel thoroughly spoiled, for there was a fire blazing in the hearth when I arrived and the room was lit to such a degree I might have imagined the midday sun was shining inside."

"I am so pleased you have brought Bess."

"How could I not? She will be so pleased to see Your Grace."

Charlotte enjoyed a comfortable tête-à-tête with her hostess until dinner was announced a short time later and she realised she was ravenous.

As they entered the dining room, a vast room that seemed overly large for the number of places laid at the table, Charlotte found that Sebastian and another gentleman were there before them.

"Allow me to introduce Frederick Downing, my man of business but, more importantly, a very old friend. Frederick, may I present the Countess of Cranleigh?"

"It is a pleasure to make your acquaintance, Lady Cranleigh, for I have heard much about you."

"You have?" said Charlotte, sounding, and feeling, somewhat startled.

"Indeed, for when the Earl passed away it fell to me to deal with the business side of things on the Duke's behalf. Naturally I also learned of your own sad circumstances. Please accept my condolences."

Charlotte inclined her head, unable to think of a suitable reply for, while she would not affect a grief she didn't feel, neither did she wish to appear cold-hearted. She was rescued by Sebastian, who said, "Yes, well, it was some time ago and it is to be hoped that Lady Cranleigh is able now to look to the future."

She cast him a grateful glance and as she sat at the table Charlotte looked around appreciatively. The walls were lined with frescoes, which she thought beautiful and fitting for such a location. She was looking forward to seeing more of this vast establishment. "This is a magnificent room!" she exclaimed.

"But not exactly suitable for an intimate supper," the Duchess said. "I had wanted us to eat in the small dining room where I usually take my meals, but my son would have it that we dine in here. I think he's trying to impress you, my dear."

"Well, if that was his intention he has certainly succeeded, but perhaps, if it would suit you better, we might during my stay be a trifle less formal."

There was a smile in the Duchess's eyes that was reflected in Charlotte's and was most certainly at the expense of Sebastian.

"Very well, I have been uncovered," he smiled, "but I could hardly be expected to miss such an opportunity to puff off my own consequence."

"As if you care for such things," said his mother.

"As you wish, in future we shall dine in the small dining room."

There was a distinct chill in the air the next morning, but nothing would serve to deter the Duchess from visiting Bess.

Charlotte, wishing them to share their time together without intrusion, suggested Sebastian accompany his mother. "I must write to my sister and will join you later if I may."

Charlotte was just coming downstairs and was wondering which room to visit in this vast mansion when Sebastian and his mother returned to the house. The contentment on the Duchess's face was clear to see and there was, it seemed, a new bloom in her cheeks.

"Come, my dear, let us go to the parlour where there is a nice fire burning in the grate," she said to Charlotte. "Sebastian, ring for some tea if you would, for I'm feeling quite cold."

"It is to be hoped you have not taken a chill, Your Grace," Charlotte said with concern as they sat down near the hearth.

"I'm sure I shall be quite well. It isn't damp. Just there is a sharp contrast between outside and in. I shall warm up shortly. Ah, and here's Sebastian … and the tea as well. Excellent."

Charlotte made no other fuss, knowing it would not be welcome and as certain as she could be that the short excursion would have done the Duchess no harm. "I'm sure I need not ask if Bess was pleased to see you."

"She has not forgotten me, that much is certain. Her nose went straight to where I used to keep a carrot in my pocket. No day began without it."

"Then it is to be hoped if the weather is fine that you will begin each day of my stay in that way," Charlotte said. Once she had drunk her tea, she asked, "Would you think me very rude if I leave you for a while? Your son has asked me to ride out with him this morning. He said there is something special he wishes me to see."

"There is indeed," Sebastian said. "I shall have the horses saddled up while you change."

"As well that you go now, my dear, for it is at this time of day that I take a short nap. I wake so early and find that by mid-morning I need to close my eyes for a while. You will, I trust, find me quite restored by the time you return."

Charlotte went to change into her riding habit while Sebastian went outside. A while later she found him with both Bess and Sable waiting for her in the courtyard.

"I do hope they have not taken cold," she said, concerned for the horses.

"Whereas I may be chilled to the bone and it would not matter," Sebastian said, laughing. "You may be sure that Jim here would have something to say if I were to allow the smallest breeze to blow on Sable."

Charlotte had not seen the lad, who was standing on the far side of the horse and hidden from view. She was astonished when he replied with a grin, "Right you are, Your Grace. A fine scolding, that's what you'd get from me."

Sebastian laughed and flicked the boy's ear with such affection that Charlotte was astonished but delighted to see this soft side of him. "Off with you now to the stud and tell Jacob, if you will, that I am bringing the Countess of Cranleigh with me."

"Countess of Cranleigh, is it? At once, Your Grace!" the boy said, and his eyes grew large and round, leaving Charlotte to wonder why her name had had such an effect on him.

They rode some distance within the boundaries of the estate but Jim, who had taken a more direct route and run like the wind, was there before them. Jacob was standing in the yard waiting to greet them, but on the arch above its entrance was a plaque which read 'Cranleigh Stud Farm'. Charlotte looked across at Sebastian as she dismounted to see that he was smiling at her.

"It is named for Ernest?" she asked.

"I didn't know how else to honour his memory. We are breeding a line in his name. We have a few foals already but the first, in my opinion, shows great promise. Come, I'll show him to you. But first allow me to introduce you to Jacob, without whom none of this would be possible."

"It's a pleasure to meet you, Lady Cranleigh," Jacob said. "The Earl never visited Gresham Hall, not since I've been here anyways, but from all his lordship says I reckon he'd have been pleased."

"I'm sure he would, and I'm anxious to see more."

Charlotte watched as not just Jim but two or three other lads crossed the yard as they went about their business. She knew now the reason for the boy's expression of surprise back at the main house. Cranleigh was a name with which he was already very familiar. And speaking of surprises, it seemed Sebastian was full of them. Had she not read Harriet's letter she would have been even more amazed, but now it appeared that the property in Wiltshire wasn't the only one that was sheltering and training all manner of urchins.

Charlotte looked enquiringly at Sebastian as Jacob moved away. "I'm surprised to see so many young boys here. My sister mentioned in one of her letters that there are several too at Cranleigh?"

"I see I must confess," he said, smiling, but at the same time there was an arrested look in his eyes. "It began many years ago. I was in London and had taken a wrong turn. I found myself in a squalid area of the city and witnessed such things as I could not believe."

"Such as?"

"They are things that are not, I think, fit for a lady's ears."

"Don't be foolish! I am not a child or so missish that I need to be sheltered from life's realities," Charlotte said, a trifle waspishly.

"Very well. The poverty was unimaginable. People begging in the street. This wasn't unexpected, of course, but I couldn't believe the cruelty that allowed a grown man to horsewhip a child with impunity."

A small gasp escaped Charlotte, but she said nothing and he continued.

"I dealt with the man, as you may well imagine, and took the boy with me to Berkeley Square, from where I sent him here to Gresham Hall. But he was only one amongst so many." Sebastian smiled again, ruefully this time. "It has become an obsession with me and a source of sorrow that I am unable to help more of his kind. But Cranleigh has enabled me to double the number of children we are able to accommodate. You would not believe the satisfaction one attains in watching them recover from their wounds. How lively they are when one would have anticipated rather that their spirit would be broken. And so, they learn a trade, in the stables, on the farm, in the smithy. And when they leave, they are equipped to make their own way in the world. But for each one that goes on his way, there are many to take his place." Sebastian seemed to come out of his reverie, aware again of Charlotte standing beside him. "But you must forgive me. I have been rambling on in an unforgivable fashion."

Charlotte merely said, "You are full of surprises. Your passion does you credit. And now perhaps you will show me this new arrival."

"He is quite beautiful!" exclaimed Charlotte said upon seeing the foal. "I can see why you are so hopeful of him. What do you call him?"

Again that slightly twisted smile. "Nothing officially yet. I am hoping that you will suggest something fitting. His stable name is Snowflake."

"But that is delightful, and suits him so well! Was it Jacob's idea?"

"No, it was Jim's, and if you ask me that boy is given far too much licence here," he said, but the smile was broader now than ever.

"Where on earth did you find him?"

"I didn't. He found me. Or rather, he found Sable. He was so taken with the horse that he followed me home and thereafter, until he was discovered, he slept in his stall."

"What! Here? At Gresham Hall?"

"No, it was in London. Frederick was checking the horses when Jim shot in, hotly pursued by a tradesman. It seemed the boy had stolen an apple."

"And Mr Downing saved him."

Something very much resembling a grin appeared on Sebastian's face. "My first encounter with Jim was in Berkeley Square. I'd returned from I don't remember where to find them both in the hall, the boy cowering in the corner, and a sorry sight he was, I can tell you."

"Lucky for him he ended up in the right place."

"Yes, but he didn't it realise at first. He's a natural with horses, though I didn't know that then, of course. But his evident interest meant he was a prime candidate to come here. In any case, I certainly wasn't going to put him back out on the streets."

"That was kind of you." Charlotte was delighted to see Sebastian so animated.

"I hope I have compassion enough not to have done something so cruel. Anyway," he continued, "poor lad thought I was going to hand him over to the law. I wish you could have heard him when I said he was to come here. 'I ain't done nothing wrong, guvnor. Really, I ain't. It's not as if I was stealing for meself. What's Gresham? It ain't prison is it?' I shouldn't smile, of course, but it was a personal delight when he changed from a terrified scrap of a boy to one who suddenly saw a whole new world opening before him. 'Not prison,' I said. 'My country home — where there are stables. And lots of horses, all in need of looking after. You will learn to look after them.'"

"It's easy to see he is completely at ease around them," Charlotte commented.

"But you must permit me to tell you what happened next. You may imagine what a state he was in, a boy from the streets, so I asked Frederick to take him away and wash him. Find him some clothes and somewhere to sleep. Even beneath all that dirt it was possible to see him turn pale. 'Do his Grace's plans for your future not suit you, Jim?' Frederick asked. 'He said wash, sir!' was his reply. 'You ain't going to put me under the pump, are you?' To which came the answer, though by this time Frederick was struggling to control his own features, 'So, soap and water are strangers to you, are they? Never mind. Come with me. You'll soon get used to them.' Fortunately for me, he then dragged him away and I was able to give vent to the laughter that was consuming me."

By this time Charlotte too was laughing. What a joy it was to her to see Sebastian in his element. When he shed his habitual dignity he was, she found, a very likable man.

The Duchess was awake and much refreshed by the time they returned. Dismissing her son after a light nuncheon, she begged to be allowed to show Charlotte the Long Gallery.

"You will be bored, I am sure, but there are one or two very fine paintings that I think you might like. My son is not the only member of the family who likes to show off," she said with a smile. "Be kind enough to give me the support of your arm."

"I am certain you have every reason to be proud," Charlotte said, and so it proved.

Occasional furniture lined one side of the room, each of the pieces set between tall windows which ran almost from floor to ceiling, and which contained folding shutters and were adorned with heavy drapes. The opposite wall was covered with paintings to suit every taste.

"I see that horses are well-represented in your collection," Charlotte said. "I admire this one in particular."

"You have a good eye, my dear. My late husband was not much interested in them, but there are many family portraits of which he was immensely proud."

"Was the late Duke a great collector?"

"Not really, for much of what you see has been accumulated down the generations. But he added pieces here and there which enhanced the whole."

Charlotte paused, unsure whether she should ask the question that rose to her lips. "Has it been many years since you were widowed, Your Grace?" she asked as gently as she could.

"Oh heavens, yes. Charles died when Sebastian was still in leading strings. We were blessed with only the one child, and it has been a source of regret to me that I never had a daughter."

"I am so very sorry."

"Oh, don't be. My horses were as children to me. The Duke will have you believe that I paid more attention to them than I did to him, but it wasn't the case. Though I was delighted, of course, when he displayed at a very early age a similar love for them. It is the same with you, I believe."

Charlotte admitted as much and told the Duchess something of her life at Stapleton where she had the freedom to ride every day. "But I have never before been lucky enough to own such a mount as Bess. I cannot thank you enough for entrusting her to me."

"Where horses are concerned, I trust my son absolutely."

"But he had never then seen me ride."

The Duchess merely smiled and changed the subject. "And how do you find life in the capital, having been raised and lived all your life in the country?"

"I enjoy it very much, but along with all its advantages it brings many restrictions."

"Restrictions?"

"Yes, for although I love the theatre and the shops are outstanding, superior even to those in Bath, and they were well enough, I feel all the while that people are looking at me."

"People will always look at you, my dear. You are a very attractive young woman."

Charlotte felt uncomfortable and tried again to explain. "Please don't misunderstand me. In spite of spending months out of circulation, I have made many friends and I value them dearly. The company is stimulating and it is that I should most miss if I were to return to Stapleton."

The Duchess looked puzzled. "Is there any prospect that you might do so?"

"Oh no. Most certainly not. It's just that, well, I can hardly stride around the streets of London as I would in the country. And I am quite a managing female. That would never go down well in town. I am used to having a job to do and sewing a sampler does not bring with it the same satisfaction." She laughed aloud. "That could, of course, be a consequence of my not being an expert needlewoman. Esther, my cousin, was always on hand if any repairs were required, and I don't have the patience to set a neat row of stitches."

"Instead you would look out the window to see who might be passing by, or wonder whether the weather was clement enough for a walk."

"You do understand," Charlotte said with a sigh of relief, for she had worried that she might be sounding rather spoiled.

CHAPTER SEVENTEEN

"I believe I made a real nuisance of myself with the farmers at Stapleton," Charlotte told Sebastian, four days later. "I could not resist the lambs, you see, and have even hand-reared one myself when its mother didn't survive."

"Are you thus with all animals?"

Charlotte looked at Sebastian and smiled. "I fear so. I cannot see one in pain, or hungry. It is more particularly so with the young ones. I suppose it comes with having been raised in the country."

"Or perhaps it is just that you have an affinity with all creatures," Sebastian said.

"I would like to think that is the case. However, there are one or two people of my acquaintance to whom I would not give the time of day."

"You might have said that of me not so long ago," Sebastian replied. "You were certainly not *aux anges* with me when we were at Stapleton."

"It is ungallant of you to bring that up when I am your guest now and beholden to you. But I admit I was put out."

"Put out! I see you are not prone to exaggeration."

"Perhaps you are right," Charlotte said with due honesty. "I was very angry, but that was before I fully understood what your plans were and that you had truly rescued my father from his own inadequacies. But I should not speak so of my parent."

"I hope you will always feel able to speak the truth to me. Whatever you tell me in confidence shall go no further, and I understand that life must have been difficult for you in the past."

Sebastian was referring to her life at Stapleton, but he could not know that with her marriage she had escaped from one kind of bondage merely to be the victim of another. Throwing off the thought, Charlotte shrugged and pointed to the small flock of sheep, remarking that it would not be long before the bleating of lambs would be heard on this farm.

During the previous few days at Gresham Hall, Charlotte had come to realise that one might spend a lifetime and not see all its splendour. Built two centuries earlier, its four wings enclosed a huge courtyard accessed by an opening in one of the sides. She had not yet been privileged to see the Royal apartments but had been rendered speechless by the splendour of the magnificent Jacobean oak screen in the great hall.

"There is no historical record that royalty ever stayed here," the Duchess had told her, "but family tradition has it that it was so."

Charlotte couldn't help smiling and thinking that Sebastian wasn't the only one capable of puffing off his consequence. One thing she did know. When the time came, she would be sorry to leave. On this beautiful estate she found herself often admiring but sometimes wistful, since she no longer had a home of her own away from the city. It was a lowering thought, but she shrugged it off as best she could, for there was no solution that she could see. It wasn't, however, easily set aside. She foresaw an unsettled future, the feeling all the more accentuated because she was enjoying her time so much at Gresham Hall.

Charlotte wrote again to Harriet. She described the situation at Gresham Hall and how it was mirrored to a large extent at Cranleigh.

There is an urchin here named Jim who, it seems, stole an apple to give to Gresham's horse, even though he was himself starving. The lad has no fear and will readily stand at a horse's hooves. They never strike out at him, though. It's funny, is it not, how animals know whom they may or may not trust? The Duchess is delightful and has shown me much of the house, though it is so vast I fear it would take half a lifetime to discover all its secrets. She took me one day to the chapel and told me that when the late Duke passed away, she had at first spent many hours there, gaining comfort from the peace of her surroundings, until she discovered that she found more solace from riding about the estate. Jester was the name of her horse then, and she speaks of him with as much affection as of Bess.

Charlotte paused, her pen held above the inkwell, before continuing. She had been on the point of telling her sister how much she longed to live again in the country, but thought better of it. Harriet was living just such a life and she did not wish to sound envious.

I am to remain here another week, when I believe the Duke must return to town and will escort me to St James's Square. It is some time since I have seen all our friends and I so look forward to meeting them again.

There, Charlotte thought, *that should suffice.*

To the surprise and delight of both Charlotte and Sebastian, the presence of a coach in the courtyard as they returned from their morning's ride two days later heralded the arrival of Cosmo Fortescue and Hector Ruthin. The travellers had already entered the house and were discussing with the chief steward the distribution of their luggage and the length of their stay.

"Ah, Gresham, there you are," Hector said. "Hope you don't mind, old boy. I've been visiting with Fortescue at his place in Berkshire, and it seemed to us both only a stone's throw to come into Oxfordshire and stay with you for a day or so before our return to town. Dauntry here is to put us in our old rooms," he said, indicating his thanks to the steward who was even then leaving the hallway. "What's that? Lady Cranleigh?" he said, seeing Charlotte as she appeared from behind the Duke.

Sebastian, evidently feeling some explanation was due, said, "The Countess has been good enough to pay a visit to my mother and is remaining for a week or so. She will be glad of your company, I am sure, for she must be truly bored with mine." He smiled and shook Hector's hand and then Cosmo's.

"It is an agreeable surprise to find you here, Charlotte," Cosmo said, turning towards her and pressing her fingers warmly.

"And it is a pleasure to see you, though I fear it is the Duke who must be bored and will be glad of some male company for a change."

"Come," said Sebastian, "let us all adjourn to our rooms to change for luncheon. It will be served in a half an hour or so and it wouldn't do to keep the Duchess waiting."

"Nonsense," replied Hector. "Never met a more easy-going woman. Her Grace and I are old friends and I am certain she wouldn't kick up a dust over a few minutes. Mind you, we have been on the road for a while and I must admit I could do with something to eat."

"I said the very same thing when first I arrived," Charlotte added, smiling at this very likeable man, whose only fault in her opinion was his terrible lack of judgement when it came to horses. She was therefore hard put not to laugh when later at the table he threw down the gauntlet to Sebastian, though it would appear that this time he had struck lucky.

"Bought Cheetham's bays, you know. Had it in mind to challenge you to a race, Sebastian. I know you don't think much of my taste, but even you will admit to them being as beautifully matched a pair as you could hope to find."

It was true, as Sebastian acknowledged. "But you will be driving them, Hector. I couldn't possibly take such advantage of you," he said.

"I am much improved since last you saw me. What do you say? Shall we race to Brighton upon our return to London?"

"Well, I expect my pair would enjoy the exercise. Yes, when we go to town I shall go to White's and see that it is entered in the book there. Do you bet against yourself?"

"Nonsense, Sebastian. I plan to beat you," he said, and tucked heartily into his meal.

"You must indeed then have improved if you think to cross the finish before my son," the Duchess said.

"Oh, I have, Your Grace. You might like to place a bet on me."

"Fond of you as I am, Hector, I think probably not."

Charlotte spent much of the following day with the Duchess while the gentlemen challenged each other in various sports about the estate.

"They are like children when they get together, are they not, my dear?" the Duchess remarked.

"It would seem so. Mr Downing told me a favourite game when he and the Duke were boys was to play knights and dragons. And now the four of them are gone out together and it wouldn't surprise me if the game has been resurrected."

"Oh, yes! They may no longer be boys but the spirit of adventure is still there."

Sophia all the while sat quietly at her sewing and Charlotte felt how sad it was that the Duchess should have as her companion one so little blessed with a sense of humour or animated conversation. She had at first felt sorry for the woman, as it had appeared she was an indigent relative to whom their hostess had given a home.

"Oh no, I have several brothers and sisters, all of whom have their own children," she had replied when Charlotte asked if she were an only child. "I am an aunt many times over and have been begged often to reside with one or other of my siblings. However, I prefer to stay with her Grace."

It was on another day, when conversation had been particularly tedious, that the Duchess had said in answer to a raised eyebrow of Charlotte's, "She believes I would be lonely without her, and I don't have the heart to send her away."

"Well, all I can say is you must have the patience of a saint. Better my own company than one who would in no time give me a fit of the blue devils."

"One can grow tired of one's own company and this is a large house. I can always escape if I feel the need. You think, like Sebastian, that because Sophia does not have a lively mind it must be tiresome to spend time with her. It isn't the case. Better a quiet companion than a chatterbox, which is something I could not bear. She looks out for me, and if the truth be known I am grateful to have her here."

Charlotte realised what a lonely life the Duchess must lead when her son was away and could readily understand why he should return to his country seat as often as he might, and she admired him for it. "I hope I don't presume too much, but you are aware, I know, that I no longer have a home in the country.

It would be a great honour if you would allow me to visit you again, from time to time. As a break from all the goings-on in town, you understand."

"You are welcome here at any time, my dear," the Duchess said.

Charlotte was enjoying herself immensely and realised she would be returning to London with very little enthusiasm. Perhaps, of the two of them, the Duchess was the more fortunate after all.

The friends extended their visit into the following week, none having any particular engagements and all enjoying the delights Oxfordshire had to offer. Cosmo and Hector returned to London only one day before Charlotte and Sebastian.

Charlotte took leave of her hostess then left the room so the Duchess might be alone with her son. He was some minutes and remarked when he came out that he hated leaving her. "But I shall return as soon as I may. Perhaps, if you have no other obligations, you might care to join me. Your time here has done her no end of good."

"Indeed I should love to. First, though, I must visit Mr and Mrs Harvey. Esther has been begging me to come and stay for a while. I think she is anxious to show me her new home."

It was the truth, and Charlotte was looking forward to joining her cousin for a while. She could not deny, however, that it cost her a pang to refuse Sebastian's invitation, for the time being at least.

The weather being fine and crisp, Charlotte regretted being confined to the carriage as she told Sebastian. "Bess and I both shall miss those long gallops about your estate. London parks are not the same."

"Perhaps we might get a party together and ride further out. I could arrange for us to take luncheon at an inn, if that would suit you."

"What a delightful idea. Yes, please do so."

They arrived back in London, each happy with the other's company and sorry to be parted.

"I shall call upon you tomorrow, if I may. Just to make sure you are settled in," Sebastian said, smiling as he handed Charlotte up the steps of her house.

"You are very good. I shall look forward to seeing you." She looked over her shoulder to see that the footman was patiently holding the door. Turning back to Sebastian, she held out both hands to him. "Goodbye, dear friend, and thank you. It was a great pleasure to see her Grace and to stay at Gresham Hall."

Charlotte was waiting in the morning room when Sebastian arrived the next day. She'd not had the audacity to don her riding habit but was hopeful he might invite her to join him in the park and was ready to change at top speed, well aware that gentlemen did not like to keep their horses waiting. She wouldn't herself. She tried not to feel disappointment when he entered, so obviously was he not dressed for riding. She was more than glad she had not taken the outing for granted.

"Good morning, Lady Cranleigh. It is a fine day, is it not?" he asked, taking her hand. "I hope I find you rested."

This cool civility was so far from how he had been addressing her of late that she wondered what she could have done to warrant such formality.

"Indeed it is, and thank you, yes, I am. So much so that I have the fidgets and had it in mind to take Bess out."

"Am I detaining you? Would you prefer me to return another time?"

His response seemed very curious. Sebastian seemed so removed from his customary urbane self that Charlotte began to feel sure she had in some way offended him and, in her straightforward way, she asked him if that was the case. He looked away, then back, then began pacing the room, before returning to where she stood and grasping her hands — rather tightly.

"I know you are too principled to play with my affections. Tell me now if I have any hope of winning your hand and heart."

Charlotte paled and moved a step back. "I don't understand. I have never given you any reason to think … you have never before displayed any sign…" She stopped, not knowing what next to say. Her heart beat fast within her breast as she at last acknowledged to herself her feelings for this man.

"I am making such a mull of this, aren't I?" Sebastian said, throwing his hand through his hair again before smiling at last in the way she had grown to love. "Dear Charlotte, I am aware that I was for long an irritation to you. I have tried hard to rectify that and in doing so have fallen deeply and enduringly in love with you."

"But you cannot have done so! We are friends, that is all. I have no thought of marriage." But her eyes belied her words.

"I know it too well, but it has been some considerable time since I have been hoping we could be much more than friends. I offered you guardianship a long while ago. It seemed to an extent that you accepted me in that role."

"I … I don't know what to say."

"If you cannot return my love, tell me now. I will leave you and never speak of this again. But if there is a chance, if I can but hope…"

Charlotte stepped forward again into the space between them. Her hands returned his grip and she looked up into his eyes. "You are aware that both my sister and my cousin have recently been married. I know, because we have been so open with each other, that you must be aware how I long for a home in the country and all the freedom that would give. I would not, I could not bear it if this was an extension of your self-imposed guardianship. Rather I would remain a widow than marry out of your pity for me."

"I have never pitied you in my life," he said vehemently and crushed her in his arms before she could protest further.

As he released her she put the tips of her trembling fingers to her lips and smiled shyly up at him.

"May I take it that is a yes?" he asked gently.

"I think so. But do reflect. I am very managing, you know, as I had occasion to tell your mother. Not one of those missish women who obeys her husband's every command. And you have been used to ruling the roost."

"I know that much already, and that there will be times when we will argue from one end of the day to the other. But we have done so already and still we have remained friends. Once and for all, Charlotte, will you marry me?"

"I will," she said, before adding with a smile, "but only because you have a beautiful home in the country."

"Wretch!"

No more was said for some time. They sat with Charlotte's head on Sebastian's shoulder, his arms encircling her, as he attempted to convince her with soft words that he had no wish, none at all, to be regarded as her uncle.

CHAPTER EIGHTEEN

"Would you be very offended if we did not announce our engagement until I have been to visit Esther? I will have to write to Harriet of course, but I should so like to tell my cousin myself."

"I would wish to claim you as my own, naturally, but I perfectly understand. In fact, I should prefer that my mother hear the news from me in person rather than by letter."

"Very well, then, for the time being it shall be our secret." Charlotte smiled adoringly up at Sebastian so he should be in no doubt of the strength of her feelings for him, naturally causing him again to take her in his arms. "Next then, I suppose, will be this race," she said when he again released her. "I have not seen the pair. Are they all that Hector claims?"

"Oh yes. He does not exaggerate. We have set a date for next Wednesday."

"I shall miss the race, then. I am planning to leave the day after next to visit Esther."

"You do not come to watch? You cannot love me!" he said, trying hard to look like an orphaned child.

"Enough to take the opportunity of doing something else whilst we must of necessity be apart, much though I would wish to see you ride into town ahead of Hector. You will win, I suppose?"

"Nothing is certain, but Hector is a good friend and a good sport. We shall have a splendid time I am sure, whatever the outcome."

The couple were finding it hard not to declare themselves to the world at large, so it was perhaps fortunate that each had much to do.

It was with a slightly forlorn feeling that Charlotte entered the carriage to embark on her journey to Hertfordshire, knowing it would be some days before they would meet again. Not one to mope, however, she soon engaged Bella in conversation, expressing excitement at the prospect of seeing Esther again. Conscious of the need to share her joy, she took the faithful abigail into her confidence, for with the need to purchase wedding clothes it would be necessary for her to know before long anyway.

"Oh, my Lady," Bella squealed, "I am that glad for you," and she proceeded to show her sentiments by jumping from where she sat opposite Charlotte and embracing her, such was the licence given to a person who had known one almost from one's cradle.

"Sit down, Bella, or you will fall over," Charlotte said, laughing and straightening her skirt as the girl almost fell back into her seat. "It is not yet announced, but I could keep it to myself no longer. We have so much to do, have we not?"

Naturally, a great part of the journey was spent in discussing future plans for the bride's wardrobe and Bella marvelled at the fact that her mistress was to become a Duchess.

In no time at all it seemed they had reached their destination. Esther and her husband lived not far out of London, near Barnet. Though it was still early in the year, the days were beginning to lengthen a little and they had the pleasure of getting there in time to take in much of their surroundings.

"What a delightful property you have," said Charlotte as she was greeted by Mr Harvey. "We were delighted to see the daffodils waving at us as we came up the drive."

"Spring will not be long in coming now, to be sure. It is such a fine day that Esther is in the kitchen garden, for we were not certain when to expect you and she will not have heard your arrival. Do come inside and I will bring her to you."

Esther, when she entered the room, exuded an air of contentment the younger had never seen in her before. She embraced Charlotte and there was strong emotion in her voice when she said, "I am so very pleased to see you. It seems an age."

"I almost wouldn't have known you, you look so well."

"I have never been so happy in my life," Esther replied, and the simplicity with which she spoke those words carried more weight than any grand exclamations. Charlotte, though anxious to make her own announcement, decided to wait a while, for this was Esther's moment. "When you are settled in, I should like to show you about the house. It has been in George's family for many generations and he is inordinately proud of it. We both are."

That much was obvious, and it was indeed a substantial building that showed evidence of the care that had been lavished upon it. Esther had not long enough been there to have been responsible for the tasteful furniture and decorations and, as Charlotte praised them, Mr Harvey's smile grew even broader.

Bella was unpacking Charlotte's trunk when Esther escorted her cousin to her bedchamber. Unable to contain herself any longer, Charlotte suggested her abigail might wish to return later. As the door closed behind her, she turned to face the woman who had been so long her wisest counsellor.

"You have news! I can tell. It is writ all over your face."

"I have, my darling. I have wonderful news. I am to be married."

"Gresham?"

"Yes! Was it so obvious?"

"Yes. Well, to me it was. Almost from the very start I have been aware that you were not indifferent to him. Had the contempt you sometimes professed to feel been real, you would not have voiced it so vehemently. It was because your emotions were engaged that you reacted when he did something you did not quite like."

"You do not like him?" Charlotte asked anxiously.

"On the contrary. I believe him to be a man of strong principles which will match your own. I cannot do more than wish you happy, which I am sure you will be."

"Oh, Esther, I am. So very happy."

Esther was agog to know all the details. When did the Duke propose? Were they at Gresham Hall at the time? Did she like the Duchess?

"Her Grace was exceedingly kind to me. I liked her excessively."

"And the proposal?"

"After we returned to London. It seems he was by no means certain I would accept."

"Remember, dearest, you gave him no encouragement. Men can be obtuse and sometimes need a little assistance."

"Well, I couldn't have given him any. I'm not certain I knew my own heart before that day."

Esther just smiled. "When is the wedding to take place?"

Charlotte explained that the betrothal was not yet public and that she had wanted to tell her cousin herself. "And I would dearly love to visit Harriet but I cannot at the moment so, now that you know, I shall write to her tonight. I wonder if she too suspects."

Esther remarked that she had little doubt of it.

"The Duke is to go to Brighton in a few days and thereafter will return home to tell his mother of our good news. I am hoping to accompany him. Not until then shall we place an advertisement in the *Morning Post*, but I believe the wedding will follow shortly afterwards."

"I am delighted it will not long be delayed, for I would wish you to be as happy as I am."

"It's as I remarked earlier. I have never before seen you in such high bloom. Now, let me not detain you, for I am aware you didn't know when to expect me and must have much to do."

"Do not worry, my dear. You shall not go hungry. But you are right. I shall go and speak to Cook and leave you to your own devices for a while." Esther paused at the door and, looking back, said, "I never thought to see all three of us so well established. I am more content for you than I can say, Charlotte, given the circumstances of your previous marriage."

"That is all past now, Esther. I shall write now to Harriet so that she may share in our joy."

My dearest sister,

I write to you from Barnet, for I am visiting with Esther and George. So welcome have they made me and such a delightful home they have that I am sure I would wish never to leave, were it not for one thing. I must return to London soon, for I AM TO BE MARRIED! Are you surprised? It seems Esther was not. But I have not yet told you the identity of my chosen partner. It is Gresham, whom you may remember me referring to not so very long ago as insufferable. I have grown to love him dearly over these past few months. Indeed, we have spent so much time together as companions that I did not myself see this coming, but Esther tells me she suspicioned it long ago. Were you the same?

The engagement is not yet made public, as I wished you and Esther to hear the news from me directly. Upon my return to town, I will be journeying again to Gresham Hall when the Duke will tell his mother of our plans. Only then will an announcement be inserted in the Morning Post, *whereafter we hope to be married quite soon and with little fuss. I will of course advise you of the date and I hope sincerely that you and Quentin will be able to join us. In the meantime, please do keep this to yourself.*

By the way, you should see Esther. She looks almost like a young girl, so happy as she is. It would seem we have all been very lucky. My love comes to you with this letter.

Your affectionate sister,
Charlotte

Early on the morning of the race, Sebastian visited the stables to check on the horses some while before they were due to be harnessed up.

"I was about to send for you, Your Grace, if you'll pardon the presumption," his groom said. "Things ain't looking too good, sir. If you'll just step this way."

Sebastian followed his man to where two magnificent black horses were stalled. Their coats, when last he had seen them, had been sleek and shiny. They were shiny still but now by reason of a covering of sweat over the whole of their bodies. And their eyes were glazed.

"What has happened here?" Sebastian asked shortly.

"They were fine as fine as could be when I looked in on them last night. This ain't normal, if you know what I mean. Not just the two of them and none of the others. If you asked me, I'd say they've been got at."

"Yes, that much is obvious. Are they in imminent danger, do you think?"

"No, Your Grace, more like they've been drugged than poisoned. I'm pretty sure they'll be okay when it wears off."

"Those are my thoughts also. Then I shall leave them with you. There is nothing for it but to locate another pair to race in their stead. Do what you can to make these two comfortable. I shall look in again on my return from Brighton."

Pausing only to check on Sable to satisfy himself his favourite had come to no harm, Sebastian strode off, his mind buzzing. There was no way Hector would have had any part in this. He would have been as horrified as Sebastian to learn of what had been afoot. Nor could Sebastian withdraw from the encounter. Too many people had placed bets and it would not be acceptable to pull back now. His first task was to find substitute horses and to wonder if they would have the stamina of his own pair to reach the posting house where he had arranged to change his team. There were not many men with whom he would trust his own horses, so he was more than grateful when Cosmo, on being applied to, immediately gave him leave to use his.

"I was just about to set off myself, as I wish to be in Brighton when you come in later. By all means have my pair harnessed to your own curricle. I shall find someone to take me up, you may be sure. This puts a different slant on the race, does it not? Not that I don't have complete confidence in my steeds, but they're not up to the pace of your blacks. Interesting. See you there."

Sebastian made it to the starting line with very little time to spare, but he was a sportsman through and through and he did not allow this setback to throw him. "Ready when you are, Hector."

"What! Are you driving Cosmo's horses?" For Hector recognised them instantly. "Where are your own?"

"Sadly incapacitated. Fortescue was good enough to loan me his for the race. Shall we go?"

"Very well. On your signal, man," Hector shouted to the starter.

A large handkerchief was dropped and both curricles leapt off the mark. Sebastian had had only minutes to get used to the feel of his pair, and he used the start of this first stretch to familiarise himself with his horses as Hector sped ahead. He smiled to himself. The bays were indeed magnificent, but in his friend's hands he feared they would be pushed too hard too soon and would be winded before ever they reached the posting house. Even on such a good road as this there would be need for caution, which Hector, flamboyant in his driving as in everything else, would likely not engage.

Sebastian saw no need to push his cattle. They were willing enough, and he felt keenly the responsibility of handling another man's horses. He was, however, a notable whip and made good steady time, arriving at the posting house only moments behind Hector. He was sad to see that the bays, already unharnessed, appeared to be winded. Certain that they would recover, he concentrated instead on his own horses, impressed by the speed with which they were changed.

He moved off behind his friend, found the measure of his pair and soon passed Hector on a straight stretch of road. There was little to do after that than savour the experience. His friend was no match for him, and even with an inferior pair he drove into Brighton while Hector was still out of sight.

There were congratulations all round as the horses were unharnessed and out of the way before Hector was seen labouring his cattle on the approach to the finish.

"I shall expect you to take me up on the way back to London so we can pick up my pair. How did you find them?" Cosmo asked Sebastian as they went arm in arm into the Old Ship on the seafront.

"So well that I may have to make you an offer for them. For now, let me get you something to drink. Ah, here comes Hector. Make that three jugs of ale, please, landlord."

"Well, that was a damned good race, Sebastian. Cosmo, I must take you on soon as well. Nothing like a good trip out into the country, eh?"

The friends, by this time ravenous, ordered some food and settled down at a small table.

Various members of their acquaintance came over to congratulate Sebastian and commiserate with Hector, for there were many who had bet on the race and had travelled to Brighton because they wanted to see first-hand what the outcome might be.

Sebastian noticed Roxburgh standing away to one side. He did not approach them but it was obvious that he had backed the loser, for nothing would have induced him to bet on Gresham.

There was no question of the friends returning to London that day and lodgings had been engaged for the night at the Old Ship. Nothing must be done the following morning but that they visit the Brighton Pavilion.

"I could fancy myself somewhere in the East, rather than in an English seaside town," remarked Cosmo. "What think you of all those domes?"

"Remarkable," said Sebastian, but there was a certain dryness in his voice and one eyebrow was raised disdainfully. "Shall we venture inside and see what delights await us?" he asked his friends reluctantly. It was evident they were both keen to go in, and he could only be grateful the Prince Regent was not in residence and there were few people to be seen there. He hoped the visit would not be of long duration.

"By Jove, yes," said Hector, who proceeded to lead the way. "I am told it's quite splendid."

Splendid it was, but such extravagance did not suit the Duke's taste. Hector loved it, though, its excesses well suiting his grandiose leanings. They were shown into the various rooms, each one even showier it seemed than the last.

"I feel I should like to walk along the Promenade to clear my head after all that splendour. What do you say?" Sebastian asked his companions, seemingly gasping for air as they came once more into the open.

Cosmo and Hector were agreeable and the three exchanged greetings with several other bucks who had chosen to do the same. One was overheard to say to his companion, "I see Roxburgh has returned straightway to London. Did you see him after the race? His face was like thunder. I believe he dipped rather deeply. One would have thought such an experienced gambler as he would have known better than to hazard his chances on Ruthin."

Fortunately, Hector's attention had been drawn by another and he did not hear this slight on his driving ability, but Sebastian could only wonder if Roxburgh had already been parted with all the money he had paid him for Sir Archibald Willoughby's gambling debts.

Bright sunlight greeted the party the next morning, a little too bright for Hector, who had partaken of a considerable quantity of wine the previous evening.

"Would you like me to drive you?" Cosmo asked, amused but concerned.

"Thank you, but I think it will do me good to have something other than my aching head to concentrate upon," he replied rather ruefully.

"Then I shall go with Gresham as planned and collect my horses. Shall we wait for you at the posting house?"

"Wait for me! Nonsense! I shall reach there before you and it is I who shall be waiting." And, having thrown down this challenge, he set off at a spanking pace, his aching head forgotten in the pleasure of the chase.

"Will he never learn?" Sebastian said, smiling and himself taking up the reins.

"Hector? With regard to horses? Never, I fear, but his enthusiasm is infectious. It is above all things what I most like about him."

"Yes, a great fellow."

With no limit on their time, they stopped for a leisurely lunch at the posting house. Cosmo's horses, and indeed Hector's bays, were harnessed up and they arrived back in London well before the light had begun to fade.

Sebastian went immediately to check on his horses and found that the pair had recovered well. There was no doubt in his mind that they had been tampered with and he felt only sadness that there were those who would commit such foul deeds.

Back in Berkeley Square, Sebastian wondered if Charlotte would return to the capital the following day as planned or if she would extend her visit to Barnet. He could not wait to take her to Gresham Hall to tell his mother their news before announcing their joy to the world at large.

CHAPTER NINETEEN

"Oh, how I've missed you!" Charlotte said, rising as Sebastian entered the morning room.

He moved towards her and embraced her before putting her at arm's length and exclaiming, "You have been constantly in my thoughts, my love. How did you find Mr and Mrs Harvey?"

"They are both well, thank you, and I have never seen Esther in such good looks. Nothing, I am sure, to do with the air," she added, smiling, "for I lived with her in the country all my life, and she was never like this before."

"Was your cousin astonished at your news? Will they come to the wedding?"

"Certainly they will. I could not be married without her, I think, for you know she has always stood as a mother to me. And, no, she was not surprised at all. It seemed she was aware that my affections were engaged long before I was myself. No, stay back," she commanded as he moved towards her with the obvious intention of again taking her into his arms. "We have much to talk about."

"Very well, but I had better warn you now that mutiny of this sort will not be acceptable once we are married."

Charlotte thought how softened his features were when he smiled. She rather suspected that he had for so long stood on his dignity and maintained his distance from people that it had become a habit. She was pleased to see it waning.

Charlotte somewhat shyly asked when he thought they might be married. He was hoping, he said, that the banns would be posted immediately upon their return from the country and that they be wed three weeks after that.

"So soon?"

"It cannot be soon enough for me, my darling. Will that be sufficient time for you to put in place any arrangements you might need to make?"

"Esther and George hold themselves in readiness. I must write to Harriet, for I do not know how difficult it is for Quentin to leave Cranleigh."

"Ingram is a good man, and things are going along so well now that your brother-in-law may absent himself at any time he wishes."

"Of course. I had for the moment forgotten you are so closely involved. But wait. What of your mother? I would not have her undertake another journey to London, for I know she felt there would be no more visits after she was so affected by the last. Could we not be married at Gresham Hall?"

Sebastian jumped to his feet and knelt in front of her, taking her hands which were clasped in her lap. "I did not care to ask you. I felt sure you would want a big affair with all your friends in attendance."

"Then you do not know me at all! I should like nothing better than a small wedding with our close family and friends about us. Could not Cosmo and Hector travel to Gresham Hall? It seemed when they were last there that it was as a second home to them. Certainly Mr and Mrs Peacock and Mr and Mrs Harvey can as easily come to Oxfordshire as to London."

Charlotte and Sebastian set off by coach the next morning to Gresham Hall. It would be a flying visit. There were some arrangements which could only be made in London.

"I feel a trifle conscience-stricken not to be bringing Bess."

"In a few weeks she will be able to stay for as long as you would wish. I'm sure my mother will be happy to forego seeing her this time when we acquaint her with the reason for our visit."

Charlotte looked at him a little anxiously. "Will she be pleased, do you think?"

Sebastian laughed aloud. "Pleased! She has been wanting me to be married since I don't know when. In any case, she adores you already. I make no bones about telling you, though I could not before for obvious reasons, that she has given me the hint more than once since first she encountered you."

"You cannot know how happy I am to have met her already, else I should be undertaking this journey in fear and trepidation."

"I hope I do not inconvenience you, Your Grace, returning so soon," Charlotte said to her hostess when they were later seated in her cosy parlour.

"Foolish girl, it must ever be a delight to see you here."

It was time, Sebastian judged, for him to enter into the conversation. Taking advantage of the fact that Sophia had absented herself from the room, he said, "That's fortunate, Mama, because you will be seeing Charlotte more than you might imagine. We have come to ask for your blessing, for we are to be married."

The Duchess looked from one to the other and said only, "My dears, I cannot tell you how happy you have made me." But her feelings were writ all over her face.

Charlotte rushed to embrace her and Sebastian, employing a delicacy so often absent in gentlemen, left them alone together.

In the few days they remained at Gresham Hall, much was accomplished. The ceremony would take place three weeks hence in the chapel where Sebastian's mother had once before taken Charlotte. With arched windows on each side, and a simple altar at its head, there was a sense of peace and light.

"I shall like to be married here," Charlotte told Sebastian, reflecting how much more appealing she found the simplicity of this place than the fashionable church where she had so unwillingly married Ernest. "But I must tell you, I am much disturbed by a conversation I had with your mother earlier."

"I cannot believe she would say anything to distress you, Charlotte."

"It was not her intention, of course, but she tells me she is resolved to move to the Dower House after we are married."

"It is usual, I believe."

"But this is dreadful," she said distressfully. "I know what it is to leave a beloved home against one's will, and I will not be the cause of that happening to the Duchess. Why, she has lived here for most of her life!"

Sebastian realised he was to have a fight on his hands, either with his betrothed or with his mother. "What then would you have her do?"

"Is it not obvious? The house is huge. The Duchess already has her own apartments. What reason could there possibly be to separate her from us? I delight in her company and I believe I am right in saying that she enjoys spending time with me. Why on earth would we forever be going back and forth when we may reside under the same roof?"

"And have you discussed this with her?"

"Of course I have not. She seems determined, and it would be impertinent to be setting up my will against hers. I came immediately to see you, for I feel sure you will be able to persuade her of the sense of my suggestion, my darling."

Sebastian wasn't sure he had such faith in his powers of persuasion. Here were two strong-willed women, each wanting to do what was right, the wishes of each apparently irreconcilable. But he loved Charlotte even more, if that were possible, for her sensibility, and how he enjoyed her spirited attitude to any obstacle she faced. Life with her would not be boring, that much was sure. But he was uncertain how best to resolve this present problem.

"If you do not object, it might be best that I speak to her alone. I appreciate your generosity and compassion, and I honour you for it," he said, taking her hands. "It is not something I would have asked of you, but your logic makes perfect sense to me. It will to my mother, I am sure, once I can bring her down from her high horse. Leave it to me. And … thank you."

"You cannot wish to be burdened with an old woman."

"You are right, of course, but I'm afraid Charlotte will not have me on any other terms. My whole future happiness rests in your hands, Mama. So you see, it is important that you agree to this or I shall lose her forever."

This was nonsense and they both knew it. The Duchess had steeled herself to leave the house she loved and was being offered a lifeline. Setting her pride aside, she grasped it willingly. "Then I have no choice but to agree. You are a very lucky man, Sebastian."

Charlotte and Sebastian returned to London, the advertisement was placed in the *Morning Post* and they received the congratulations of their friends and acquaintances. Much of the bride's time in the ensuing days was spent choosing dresses and hats and shoes. Trying to stand still when undergoing the first fitting for her wedding gown proved to be an almost impossible task.

"Please refrain from fidgeting, your Ladyship, or this hem will be all over the place," said the dressmaker, but her voice was full of amused understanding.

"I cannot help but twist and turn, for I want to see every part of it."

"And so you shall, but all in good time."

Charlotte left the dressmakers and was about to proceed to her next appointment when a coach and four approached her. Before she had time to react, a blanket was thrown over her and she was bundled inside.

She heard a man cry, "We have our prize. You know the way. Towards Osterley. Off you go, man," and the coach pulled off.

Inside the coach Roxburgh removed the cover that was holding Charlotte in its folds. When she saw who her captor was, her overriding emotion changed in a moment from terror to fury.

"You! I had not thought even you would sink this low," she spat breathlessly.

Roxburgh spoke in a companionable tone. "If I could not have you by fair means, it was necessary that I use foul. Make yourself comfortable, my dear. We have a long journey ahead of us."

Once Charlotte had taken stock of the situation she made no attempt to struggle, or to shout and scream. It would be useless, she realised and, as a cold anger overwhelmed her, she knew it was imperative she keep her wits about her. By the time Sebastian went to their usual meeting place she would be long gone, and no one would know where. Only her own shrewdness could save her now. "I trust, if you are to carry me to Gretna, that you have provided me with at least a change of clothes."

"Do not worry. We don't go that far. We shall reach our destination in little more than two hours."

Was he so sure of himself that he did not feel the need to cloud the issue? At least she was reassured that he did not mean to carry her the length of the country. Though there could hardly be any doubt, she felt it best to ascertain exactly what his motives were.

"Am I to assume that by kidnapping me, you think that you can force me into marriage, my Lord?"

"There will be no need to use force. You will marry me gladly in a day or so."

Charlotte did well to conceal her fear, but inside she was terrified. "And does the fact that I am betrothed to another mean nothing to you?"

"Nothing whatsoever. Even had you not agreed to marry Gresham I would have continued in my pursuit of you. I do not give up easily. Your engagement merely precipitated an action which is as repugnant to me as it must be to you."

Every instinct was to scream at him but she maintained a calm she was far from feeling. "I doubt that very much."

"Charlotte, I have loved you almost from the first. I will admit, for I am basically a sincere man, that in the beginning it was your fortune I desired. But very soon you captivated me. I am truly bewitched. Understand, if you will, my position. You are the woman with whom I would spend the rest of my life. You are rich. I am, financially speaking, a broken man. If I can but have you, I would have nothing left in life to wish for."

"And what will the rest of the world say when they know already that I am promised to Gresham?" Just saying his name gave her courage.

"They will say nothing, if you value your reputation, for you will tell this world you worry so much about that you were mistaken in your affections and have changed your mind."

There was heat in his voice and Charlotte pressed herself into the corner of her seat, her flesh creeping, almost overwhelmed with horror. She forced herself to breathe deeply, to calm herself, for she needed to think.

Sebastian looked up in surprise from the table where he was studying some documents as Jim rushed towards him.

"What is it? What has happened?"

Jim struggled for breath. "It's her Ladyship, sir. He's took her," he managed, before standing there panting and clutching his arms across his belly. "I was running errands for you, sir, and I saw her get taken in a coach. I'm sure it was her, sir."

"Was there any identification on the carriage? A crest, anything of that kind?" Sebastian asked.

"No, sir, not that I saw anyways."

Sebastian groaned.

"But I sees who it was and I hears what he said. He called out to the driver. Osterley, he said. I ain't never heard of the place, but I remembers it clear because it sounded like hostelry."

"Roxburgh!" Sebastian said. "You have done well, boy. Now, if you have breath left in you, run to the stables and tell them to order my curricle immediately. You will come with me and be able to identify the carriage if we are able to overtake it."

CHAPTER TWENTY

On reaching Roxburgh's country home, they were greeted by the Viscount's housekeeper. The servant showed Charlotte to her allotted chamber, but Roxburgh followed them up the stairs to his own room and she had no opportunity of appealing to the woman for help. It was evident from all that she found as she closed the door behind her that Roxburgh indeed meant to keep her there until he had broken down her resolution. Brushes and beauty products adorned the dressing table, dresses were hung up and various items of apparel were neatly folded in the dresser. The sight of it all gave Charlotte a hollow feeling in her stomach.

Taking a few minutes to collect her thoughts, smooth down her gown and gather what courage she could, she descended to the dining room where her tormentor was waiting. A meal had been laid out for them, for it was well past the time for luncheon, and she sat down with seemingly not a care in the world and forced herself to choose from the dishes on offer with a semblance of enjoyment. Roxburgh was not to know that each mouthful tasted like ashes.

"You seem unperturbed, madam. I congratulate you."

Charlotte ate slowly and deliberately, using whatever tactics she could draw upon to prolong the repast, for the only thing she could hope to do at this stage was buy time.

"You have an excellent chef," she remarked, feeling that engaging her captor in conversation was preferable to further antagonising him by her silence.

"When we are married, you shall sample as many of his dishes as you wish."

The vision of her future that his words conjured up was so repugnant that Charlotte could not respond. Roxburgh was drinking steadily, and this increased her apprehension. She knew only too well that men in their cups behaved with a shameful lack of self-control.

The effect of the wine was becoming obvious as Roxburgh seemed to grow ever more reckless. Dismissing his servants, he chose to fill Charlotte's glass himself. He plucked her from the chair as if she were no heavier than a scrap of cloth and tried to pull her into his arms.

Then he turned his head sharply, as if listening, for there was the sound of a carriage sweeping onto his drive. Roxburgh cursed.

Charlotte, heart pounding, felt a rush of hope and prayed she might have an opportunity to throw herself upon the mercy of the unknown callers. Ordering her to stay where she was, Roxburgh locked the door behind him and pocketed the key. He went himself to see who called.

One punishing right from Sebastian sent him sprawling unconscious to the floor. Sebastian stepped over him hastily, leaving Jim to follow in his wake.

"Charlotte! Charlotte? Where are you?"

"In here, Sebastian, in here," she called imploringly from the dining room. Putting his shoulder to the door, Sebastian forced the lock open and found his love clinging to the table for support. "Thank God, thank God you have come! How did you know where to find me?" Charlotte said, throwing herself into his arms. Her strength at last deserted her, and she burst into tears.

Sebastian led her to a chair and bade her sit down, kneeling in front of her, murmuring soothing endearments and chafing her hands. "I will be all right presently," she said, gulping and sniffing at the same time. "He hasn't … he didn't…"

"Take your time. He cannot hurt you now."

It took a while, but when she had composed herself she asked again, "How came you to be here?"

Sebastian indicated Jim, who was standing guard behind a chair to which Roxburgh had been bound. Roxburgh's head slumped to one side. "We have young Jim here to thank for your deliverance. It was he who saw you being abducted."

Charlotte turned gratefully towards Jim and praised him liberally for his prompt action. As she did so, Roxburgh stirred and came to his senses. He struggled at first until, realising he was tied fast, gave up the attempt. An ugly sneer distorted his features as he looked at Sebastian. "You!" he said, in a voice of loathing.

"Naturally. Surely you did not think you could steal my affianced wife from me without hindrance? For what you have put the Countess through this day, you may be glad that I have not run you through. Certainly the world would be a better place without you. However, I will give you a choice. You will be tried for your crimes and the law will run its course or you may, if you elect to do so, leave this country and never return. Mark my words, though. If you choose the latter option, should you ever come back I will personally see to it that the full weight of the legal system is brought to bear against you. Come, Charlotte. Let me take you home."

Despite the mildness of the evening, Charlotte was shivering as Sebastian handed her up into the carriage. He laid a blanket over her knees but was unable to do more. Much as he would have liked to hold her in his arms and comfort her, he was occupied with his horses. "There, my darling. Keep as warm as you can and I will cover the distance as fast as may be."

A night's rest did much to restore Charlotte's shattered nerves, though when Esther arrived in the afternoon she sobbed in her arms, feeling like a child again. When three days later word arrived to report that Roxburgh was aboard a boat for France, she began fully to relax.

Two weeks later, Charlotte and Sebastian arrived at Gresham Hall to find the Duchess had been busy in their absence. With only forty-eight hours to go, the green room was decked out exactly as the bride would have wished, and Charlotte was thrilled.

"Is there such a thing as tasteful splendour, Your Grace, for it seems to me that is what you have achieved."

"I am so glad you like it. The only thing that spoiled it a little was that you were not here to enjoy it with me. I have had so much delight in it. The poor servants have been driven to distraction by the number of times I have changed my mind about where something ought to be positioned."

"I too have been driving others to distraction. The poor milliner, for example. I lost count of the number of hats I ordered or the alterations I asked her to make to them."

"I expect she will have been more than jubilant, for where you go, Charlotte, others will follow. Your hair must set off even the plainest arrangement. You have but to be seen in one of her creations and customers will flock to her door. Nor will she be above telling others that she is the Duchess of Gresham's milliner. I am sure she would have been happy to make three times the number of alterations to gain your custom. Are you to unpack your whole trousseau before the wedding? May I see what you have brought with you?"

"Indeed you may; I've been longing to show you all my pretty things. I barely knew what to choose and showed very little restraint, for I was so excited."

The Duchess smiled fondly at her and the two women spent a considerable time in Charlotte's room going through her purchases, unwrapping first one parcel and then another until the floor was littered with paper. There was one neatly wrapped package which she handed to the Duchess. "This is for you. A small gift for a very great debt."

"You owe me nothing, my dear. You have brought sunshine into my life. Am I to open it now or later?"

"Now, if you please."

The shawl of cream lace was exquisite, and the Duchess exclaimed with excitement as she drew it from the folds of paper and placed it around her shoulders.

"We may have little opportunity in the next few days to be alone, so I will say here and now, Charlotte, that you have made an old woman very happy and I thank God for sending you to us."

Nothing more was said, for it was unnecessary. The bond between the two women grew hourly stronger and, with Harriet married and Esther no longer at hand to be her mentor, Charlotte knew she was fortunate indeed in finding such a woman as her Grace to be her mama-in-law. To guide her steps into the future as a new Duchess. To be a companion whom she could honour and respect.

"Harriet! Quentin! You cannot know how excited I am to see you. How well you both look," Charlotte said when her sister and brother-in-law arrived the next day. Sebastian pumped Quentin's hand and planted a token on Harriet's cheek, at which she blushed becomingly.

"Come, you must allow me to make you known to her Grace," Charlotte said to her sister, dragging her towards the parlour where the Duchess awaited the arrival of her guests. The men hung back for a few moments, discussing some matters pertaining to Cranleigh, before joining the ladies.

"Good day to you, Your Grace. I hope I find you in good health."

"Thank you, I feel extremely well, Quentin, and it is good to see you again. It has been too long. I have just been talking to your lovely wife. It seems you are well settled in Wiltshire."

"Indeed we are, Your Grace. Are you expecting many guests?"

"Only family and close friends, but it is surprising even so how the numbers mount up. The house has not been this busy for many years, and frankly I am loving every moment."

Mr and Mrs Peacock's arrival was closely followed by that of Esther and George and, an hour later, by Sir Archibald Willoughby. His daughters greeted him respectfully but not enthusiastically, which he did not appear to notice. There were a few moments, however, when Charlotte found herself alone with her father.

"Well, my dear, it seems you are to be happy after all." She almost retorted that it was no thanks to him when it occurred to her suddenly that here was a man who had not the strength of character to make his own life a happy one. It was not possible for him to feel the love and affection that had bound her so closely to her sister and cousin, and now to Sebastian, so she replied only, "I am, Papa. I am," and resolved to think more kindly of him in the future.

Frederick, whose task it had been to organise the table, had placed Sir Archibald at the Duchess's left hand during supper and she was skilful enough to ensure he passed a pleasant evening. The following day brought Hector and Cosmo, and also Lord and Lady Stanford.

"What say we have one more game of knights and dragons?" Sebastian asked the gentlemen, a boyish grin suffusing his face, and he dragged everyone except Sir Archibald away to initiate Mr Harvey into the game. Maria renewed her acquaintance with Gresham's mother and the older man spent the afternoon in quiet reflection. With the cares of Stapleton removed from him, his younger daughter established and Charlotte about to marry a Duke, Sir Archibald was as proud and content as it was possible for him to be.

"We have had so little time together these last few days, Charlotte," Sebastian told her later when they managed to capture a few quiet moments on the terrace.

"There has been so much to do, but how I have enjoyed everyone's company. I shall be sorry when they all have to leave."

"What! When all I can think of is spending time alone with you," he said, looking a little startled.

"You know what I mean," she said, blushing becomingly. "After tomorrow, though, we shall have all the time in the world."

Charlotte stood outside the door to the chapel the next morning, her hand resting on her father's arm. A cheer went up, for the staff were waiting respectfully to greet them. Many called out their congratulations. All at once the doors were flung open and everyone rose as Sir Archibald led his beautiful daughter down the aisle. She was delighted to see that cushions in the exact shade of green she liked covered the pews. They had not been there the last time she had entered the chapel, and she hoped she would remember later to thank her mama-in-law for such a considerate touch. Then all other thoughts fled from her mind, for her eyes were drawn to the man waiting for her as she moved forward. His appearance was as exquisite as ever, his tightly fitting clothes a credit to his figure as well as his tailor. But it was his face that held her. Such a look of affection softened those once harsh features, and she knew well it was reflected in her own. She moved to his side and her father took her hand and placed it in Sebastian's own. They turned together to face the vicar, secure in their love for each other and ready to embrace the future as one. Freddy handed over the rings and they made their vows confidently and clearly.

Sebastian took her hand and kissed it gently. One intimate look that was both a promise and an acknowledgement passed between them, before they moved down the aisle together and into the courtyard. The relatives and guests who had followed them from the chapel then surrounded the couple to add their own felicitations before the Duke took his bride's arm for the short walk to the main house and on to the reception.

"How beautiful you look, my Duchess. Look how our people have taken you to their hearts." Indeed, as Charlotte looked around, the way was lined with those tenants who had come from all corners of this vast estate to welcome their new mistress. She felt humbled, aware of her new responsibilities and seeing Jim amongst the crowd, she resolved to do everything she could to aid her husband in his endeavours to help those less fortunate than themselves. They reached the house where a sumptuous breakfast awaited them, but before entering they once more acknowledged the support of their staff. Then, hand in hand and shoulder to shoulder, they turned and stepped into their new life, together.

A NOTE TO THE READER

Dear Reader

I hope you have enjoyed reading *The Reluctant Bride* as much as I enjoyed writing it. In a world that is almost unrecognisable from the one we lived in when I first submitted this book to Sapere, it's a joy to escape into another age. The Regency world has been my go-to genre in times of stress, and I hope that for a few hours I have been able to distance you from these troubled times. It hasn't all been bad, though. Zoom's ability to connect us to so many others has been a lifeline for many, and the ingenuity of people to improvise and bring things into our homes that we would not otherwise have seen is frankly, to me, astounding. Social media too has become a larger part of my life, both on a personal and professional level, and brought me closer to family and friends.

As the days grow longer, I'm looking forward to spending time in the garden. Last year I treated myself to a fabulous rattan chair, and when the sun shines I can be found sneaking out to lose myself in some other writer's realm. I say sneaking because I can't help feeling guilty when I read during the day but hey, I can always write in the mornings or when the sun goes down, and the benefits are unquantifiable.

There are three more Regency historical romances coming soon from Sapere and I've managed to crash one laptop creating more, but that's another story, though it was more like a nightmare at the time.

It seems as though there is some light at the end of the tunnel, albeit a long tunnel. In the meantime, be safe and well.

If you would consider leaving a review on **Amazon** or **Goodreads**, it would be much appreciated, though I would be just as happy if you'd like to join me on my **Facebook author page** for a chat. You can also visit me on **Twitter**, **Instagram** and my **website**.

Natalie

nataliekleinman.com

Sapere Books is an exciting new publisher of brilliant fiction and popular history.

To find out more about our latest releases and our monthly bargain books visit our website:
saperebooks.com

Printed in Great Britain
by Amazon

26398346R00119